Never in her life had a man held her hand.

Not like this, palm against palm, fingers laced. The most Josie had ever experienced was a man's hand wrapped around her gloved fingers as they danced. She'd never felt the heat that not only engulfed her hand but shot up her arm to spread all over her body. Her heart began to race—

"Josie?"

"Hmm?" As she tried to shake off the curious sensation, she took one more step than Buck did, which landed her smack up against him. Startled, she glanced up into eyes the deep blue color of the Mediterranean water surrounding her island home.

"Meet me here after I ride. I'll buy you a dog and a beer."

What should she say? What should she do? None of the etiquette rules covered an invitation for dogs and beer. Of course they didn't, because princesses didn't get into situations like this.

But did wives?

Dear Reader,

Compelling, emotionally charged stories featuring honorable heroes, strong heroines and the deeply rooted conflicts they must overcome to arrive at a happily-ever-after are what make a Silhouette Romance novel come alive. Look no further than this month's offerings for stories to sweep you away....

In *Johnny's Pregnant Bride*, the engaging continuation of Carolyn Zane's THE BRUBAKER BRIDES, an about-to-be-married cattle rancher honorabl claims another woman—and another man's baby—as his own. This month's VIRGIN BRIDES title by Martha Shields shows that when *The Princess and the Cowboy* agree to a marriage of convenience, neither suspects the other's real identity...or how difficult *not* falling in love will be! In *Truly, Madly, Deeply*, Elizabeth August delivers a powerful transformation tale, in which a vulnerable woman finds her inner strength and outward beauty through the love of a tough-yet-tender single dad and his passel of kids.

And Then He Kissed Me by Teresa Southwick shows the romantic aftermath of a surprising kiss between best friends who'd been determined to stay that way. A runaway bride at a crossroads finds that *Weddings Do Come True* when the right man comes along in this uplifting novel by Cara Colter. And rounding out the month is Karen Rose Smith with a charming story whose title says it all: *Wishes, Waltzes and a Storybook Wedding*.

Enjoy this month's titles—and keep coming back to Romance, a series guaranteed to touch *every* woman's heart.

Mary-Theresa Hussey

Mary-Theresa Hussey
Senior Editor

Please address questions and book requests to:
Silhouette Reader Service
U.S.: 3010 Walden Ave., P.O. Box 1325, Buffalo, NY 14269
Canadian: P.O. Box 609, Fort Erie, Ont. L2A 5X3

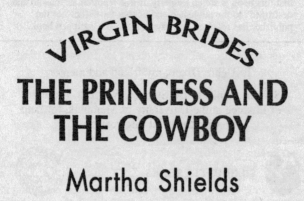

VIRGIN BRIDES

THE PRINCESS AND THE COWBOY

Martha Shields

Silhouette

ROMANCE™

Published by Silhouette Books

America's Publisher of Contemporary Romance

To Debra Dixon, my friend and mentor

Special thanks to Dr. Stephen W. Pruitt, Professor
of Finance at the University of Memphis, for help
with financial information.

 SILHOUETTE BOOKS

ISBN 0-373-19403-X

THE PRINCESS AND THE COWBOY

Visit us at www.romance.net

Printed in U.S.A.

Books by Martha Shields

Silhouette Romance

*Home Is Where Hank Is #1287
*And Cowboy Makes Three #1317
*The Million-Dollar Cowboy #1346
Husband Found #1377
The Princess and the Cowboy #1403

*Cowboys to the Rescue

MARTHA SHIELDS

grew up telling stories to her sister to pass time on the long drives to their grandparents' house. Since she's never been able to stop dreaming up characters, she's thrilled to share her stories with a wider audience. Martha lives in Memphis, Tennessee, with her husband, teenage daughter and a cairn "terror" who keeps trying to live up to his Toto ancestry. Martha has a master's degree in journalism and works at a local university.

You can keep up with Martha's new releases via her web site, which can be reached via the Harlequin/Silhouette author page at www.romance.net.

Dear Reader,

VIRGIN BRIDE. Such a notion may seem archaic in today's world, and virginity irrelevant. Virgins older than eighteen are regarded as rare at best and bizarre at worst.

Yet...think of the strength of character it takes to remain a virgin. Graphic sex is depicted blatantly on television, in movies—even in commercials. On top of this, the peer pressure urging a young woman to lose her innocence is enormous.

Even so, VIRGIN BRIDES do still exist. There are young women who believe in themselves so strongly, who are so committed to the family they one day will have, that they resist all the pressures today's world exerts. It's this kind of strength, this kind of courage that makes women heroines.

To all of the women who are or will be or once were VIRGIN BRIDES, I salute you!

Love to all,

Martha Shields

Chapter One

"**Y**ou've got to help me find a husband!"

Princess Joséphene Eugénie Béatrix Marguerite Isabeau Francoeur didn't try to hide the desperation in her voice as she locked the bedroom door of her American friend, Melissa Porter, behind them. She didn't want to chance Madame Savoie—the dragon lady who doubled as her maid—walking in on them.

The princess had visited Melissa often enough here at the prosperous Porter ranch outside Auburn, California to feel at home in any room in the two-story house, but Melissa's room was where they'd been solving their problems for over ten years. She was counting on that now.

When she turned, however, her redheaded friend's green eyes were wide with shock. "Husband? I'm the one who'll have a husband, Josie. You're here for my wedding, remember? Maid of honor. That ring a bell?"

Josie. Though she'd thought of herself by the nickname ever since Melissa first used it when they became roommates at an exclusive British boarding school, her friend was the only one who called her that. The sound felt good in her ears—like she'd come home.

But home was half a world away. Slightly larger than Martha's Vineyard, her tiny island country—officially called the Principality of Montclaire—lay in the Mediterranean, a hundred and thirty-eight kilometers off the southern coast of France.

"No, my mind is still where it always was." Josie sat on the king-size bed and tucked a leg underneath her. "What's more, he has to be rich—I'm talking in the *Forbes* top five hundred—and we have to find him before your wedding. I can't go home until I'm married."

"Find a filthy-rich husband? In five days? For a princess? Are you nuts?" Melissa plopped onto her bed. "All right, spill it. What's Bonifay done this time?"

Gilbert Bonifay was the chief minister of Montclaire. Richelieu in modern clothing.

"He's found an ancient law, made by Louis Francoeur himself. It seems my ancestor's son was fonder of men than women, if you understand my meaning. Prince Louis passed the law to force him to marry, to secure heirs to the throne."

"What is this law?" Melissa asked.

"Heirs to the throne have to marry by their twenty-fifth birthday."

Melissa's jaw dropped. "That's only three weeks away. Why hasn't Bonifay brought this up before now?"

"He says it's because Montclaire's economy is in such shambles—which it is. But I think it's mostly so he can exercise his control over me."

"I bet he already has a husband picked out for you, doesn't he?"

Josie swallowed hard, but it didn't rid her of the bitter taste in her mouth when she thought of her fiancé. "His name is Alphonse Picquet. He's the fifth richest man in France. He prides himself on having worked his way up in

Marseille from an *arrimeur*... What is the word in English?"

Melissa wrinkled her nose. "Stevedore."

Josie grabbed her friend's hand. "He's older than my father, Melissa. He's big and fat and bald and ugly—and he's going to ruin Montclaire."

"Ruin it? How?"

"One of the shepherds overheard his men talking at the north end of the island. They've found a rich supply of marble. When Monsieur Picquet becomes prince, he's going to quarry it. His surveys discovered that nearly the entire island is made of top-grade stone. In twenty years, Montclaire will be one huge pit."

"And I'm sure he'll make Bonifay rich in the process. What a sneaky, rat-faced..." Melissa peered at her closely. "You did check this out, right? There really is such a law?"

Josie nodded miserably. "It was in the historical archives, in a dusty book of law dated 1437."

"Tell me one thing. If the Princess of Montclaire is getting married, why isn't the story all over the television and newspapers?"

"I convinced my father to keep Bonifay from making the announcement until after I returned. I told him how impolite it would be to upstage your wedding. Appearances, you know." Josie smiled sadly. Appearances were all her father cared about. "It was the only concession I could get."

"Dang." Melissa shook her head in disgust. "You do need a husband, don't you?"

"It's my fault. After I graduated, I should've insisted on taking the reins of government. I should've wrested them away from Bonifay. But you know how much I hate being a princess. I was content to spend the days with my horses. I told myself I didn't know the first thing about ruling. I've never been taught the most rudimentary procedures. Bonifay saw to that. It wasn't hard for him to convince Papa I'd be

more valuable as Montclaire's window dressing. That's all
I've been—a well-dressed *objet d'art,* trotted out on special
occasions to represent my country.''

"Don't beat yourself up over it, Josie. You couldn't have
known. It's your father's fault, not yours. He's the prince.''

Tears burned Josie's eyes as she thought of her father.
Poor befuddled man. He'd spent the last twenty years in a
fog of grief, staring at the deep blue depths of the sea that
had claimed the life of her mother. His black hair had turned
to silver that very night, some said. She had to admit it
heightened his royal appearance.

Appearance was all there was to her father, though. He
would rouse himself from his grief long enough to talk to
visiting dignitaries—because that was for appearances. But
that's all he'd do. Ruling the country held no interest for
him. *She* held no interest for him. His only child.

So Bonifay was the de facto Prince of Montclaire.

"If only I hadn't been such a coward, I would've done
something before now. I would've found a rich husband
who would help my people, not make their home a rock
pit.''

Melissa grabbed her shoulders. "Don't worry, Josie.
We'll find you a rich husband. Dad's invited some of his
business friends to the wedding. He's not just a rancher, you
know. You have to invest in more than cows these days,
just to keep the cows in feed. Anyway, if one of them won't
do, surely they'll know someone who will.''

Josie hugged Melissa close and felt a weight lift from her
heart. Ever since Bonifay informed her three days ago of
the marriage he'd planned, she'd been counting the minutes
until she arrived in California. She knew the only true friend
she'd ever had would help her.

"Are you sure this is going to work?'' Josie tugged at
the outrageous blond wig Melissa had yanked down over
her black hair.

"No," her friend said. "But do you have any other choice?"

Josie sighed. "You were just married. I'm supposed to be helping you change. Not the other way around."

"You did. It took exactly nine minutes for me to step out of my wedding gown and into this dress." Melissa waved her concerns away. "I'm ready to go. Now we have to make sure you are."

Her heart beating dully with dread at what she had to do, Josie studied her reflection in her best friend's dresser mirror. A stranger stared back at her. "I look like…like…"

"Like trailer-park trash? This is perfect. You look enough like my cousin Betty Jo to pass right by your bodyguards." Melissa scrutinized Josie's image in the mirror. "The Versace gown detracts from the trailer trash image, I know, but that doesn't matter, since it's what all eleven of the bridesmaids were wearing. It being a different color from yours will help fool them. Just remember—don't let them get a good look at your face, and giggle all the way to the stables. Like you're going there to have hot sex with a man."

Josie had long ago stopped blushing when Melissa mentioned hot sex with a man. Sex was one subject her friend never tired of. And to tell the truth, Josie liked hearing her talk. After all, sex once-removed was better than no sex at all.

Josie met her friend's eyes in the mirror. "Are you sure I'm doing the right thing?"

Melissa stopped fussing with the wig, pushed Josie's excess skirts out of the way, and sat down next to her on the dresser bench, facing her. "We've talked and talked and talked, and haven't been able to come up with a better plan. If only Dad knew more bachelors—but I guess most of the people his age are married. And the younger ones are all living on their parents' money or have jobs, so they won't do. If only we'd had more time, I could've—"

"You couldn't help it." Josie hugged her friend. "The wedding parties were already planned. You couldn't miss one given in your honor."

Melissa smiled wryly. "You don't think they were in *my* honor, do you? Most of them were an excuse for Sacramento society to get a princess into their homes."

"I'm sure that's not the—"

"That doesn't matter. What does matter is that you find a husband so you don't have to marry that awful man Bonifay picked out for you. Since we couldn't find you a decent husband in the past week, you have to find an indecent one." Melissa grinned at her own wordplay. "A cowboy will be perfect."

Josie shook her head. "I have to ask some cowboy to marry me? Who came up with this plan?"

"I did, and you know it." Melissa arched a brow. "Don't go soft on me now. It's perfect. There's a rodeo starting in a little over an hour on the south border of our property. I showed you where yesterday, when we went riding. A cowboy will be the least likely person to know who you are, plus he'd be the least likely person anyone would suspect you of marrying."

"I don't know if I have the nerve to walk up to a stranger and ask him to marry me. What if I can't find a man who will?"

"Well, don't just walk up to one and blurt it out. Ease into it. And don't worry. These are rodeo cowboys. They don't like to be tied down, but they do like money. Since you can offer the right candidate several thousand dollars in exchange for a few months' use of his name, you'll have more takers than you can throw a lasso at. Especially since this is not going to be a platonic relationship."

Josie ignored her friend's playful nudging. She wasn't thrilled with the idea of having sex with a perfect stranger, even if he would be her husband. But she knew if the marriage wasn't consummated and Bonifay's men found her, it would be quickly annulled and the wedding with Picquet would proceed.

"If only I could go with you *and* go on my honeymoon." Melissa sighed. "I could help you pick out a real cute cowboy."

Josie shook her head. "I need to do this on my own. I'm going to have to disappear for a few weeks, and I don't want even you to know where I am." Steeling herself for what she had to do, Josie took one last look in the mirror. She straightened the bodice of the gown and stood. "I'm sure Peter's getting anxious for you to go downstairs so you two can leave. You put the bundle of clothes and money in the tack room, right?"

"Behind the second row of saddles on the left." Melissa stood and faced her, tears shining in her green eyes. "Well, who'd a' thought? I'm married, and you're about to be."

Josie smiled wryly. "With any luck."

Melissa gathered her into her arms. "Take care of yourself, okay? You've never been on your own. I'll be worried."

"Don't be." Josie returned the hug. "I'll be fine. Go on downstairs. I'll slip out during the excitement of you and Peter going away."

With one last hug and a lingering glance from the door, Melissa left. A few minutes later, Josie heard the commotion of the wedding guests wishing the new couple well. She took a deep breath and slipped into the empty hall.

She grabbed a bottle of champagne and a couple of glasses as she passed the kitchen. Accessories to complete her disguise. With another deep breath, she opened the door and stepped boldly through.

What was probably less than a minute seemed like an hour, but she made it into the stable without raising an alarm. She paused to catch her breath as she entered the cool shade, but didn't linger.

Placing the champagne on a bale of hay, she picked up her voluminous skirts and ran down the wide corridor between the stalls that housed dozens of blooded thoroughbreds and quarter horses. The familiar smells and sounds of the stable comforted her, but she didn't pause to enjoy the rare solitude. She ran straight for the tack room.

Kicking her skirts aside, she reached behind the second row of saddles on the left. No bundle.

Concerned, she began pulling saddles from their racks to look behind them. No bundle. Anywhere. One of the hands must have found it, and either returned it to the house or stolen it.

Alarm blared through her. What was she going to do now? She didn't have any money or any clothes except the gown.

She forced herself to breathe, to fight the panic making her heart race. What should she do? Give up? Go back to Montclaire and marry Alphonse Picquet? Watch the bedrock ripped from her island, slab by slab?

No, that's the one thing she couldn't do.

Josie glanced down at her clothes. The skirt was full. She could ride in it. And she was wearing diamond earrings and a necklace she could exchange for American dollars.

She had to go through with her plan. Though it was ripping apart at the seams, it was the only option she had.

"Yes, ma'am." Buck Buchanan rolled his eyes toward the gray metal ceiling of the camper on the front end of his horse trailer. Why couldn't his mother just forget he existed?

"Now, Hardin, I'm counting on you coming home tomorrow night. It's your father's birthday, after all, and you know how I hate an uneven table. Besides, Susan needs an escort.''

He didn't know which he hated worse—his mother calling him by the name she'd given him at birth, or the fact that she'd set him up again with some California debutante she wanted him to marry.

"Tomorrow night? Sorry. No can do. I'll be heading for—"

"You have to, Hardin. You're giving the party."

"I'm what?"

"I'm at the ranch right now." There was a definite shudder in her voice. "How do you think I got your number this time? I found the cell phone bill in your file drawer."

Buck ground his teeth so hard he could hear the enamel scraping against itself. His parents—his mother especially—hated the Double Star Ranch. To them, it represented their ranching roots, which they'd worked as hard as any ditchdigger to "rise above." That his mother was giving his father's party at the ranch Buck had inherited from his grandfather, instead of their three-million-dollar mansion in Sacramento, meant she was stepping up her campaign to get him married.

He knew why. It wasn't because she wanted grandkids to pamper. Oh, no. His thirtieth birthday was just around the corner, and it galled her that he hadn't cemented the Buchanans' place among the California elite by marrying some rich American princess.

Like Susan. He knew her and dozens like her. Spoiled, selfish, with hair, skin and nails as perfect as the best salons could make them. They'd never done a lick of work in their lives, and would be horrified at the suggestion they ought to.

"Hardin. I'm counting on you."

That's all his mother had to say—those four little words, in that half-hurt, half-disbelieving tone of voice. She was his mother, after all. Even though she vehemently disapproved of the cowboy life he lived, he loved her.

He sighed heavily, not caring whether she heard it or not. "I'll be there."

She sighed happily, as if she'd doubted the outcome of her call. Like he'd ever been able to refuse her. His mother was a master at applying guilt. It was amazing how much she could heap on him with a dainty silver teaspoon.

"I'll see you tomorrow night."

"Goodbye, son."

Buck didn't reply. He pushed the End button on his cell phone and hurled it onto the camper bed set high on the gooseneck portion of the trailer.

Why had he answered the damn phone? He should've known it wouldn't be his lawyer this late. But he'd been distracted after checking the Internet for the day's stock prices. He'd picked it up without thinking.

Now he was stuck—not only with a damn dinner party, but with his parents' presence at his ranch. No telling how long his mother would stay if she was determined to get him married by the time he turned thirty.

He shoved open the flimsy camper door so hard it banged against the side of the trailer. He dropped to the ground in one step, bypassing the fold-down step leading up to the tiny cramped quarters he called home most of the year. The two-inch slanted heel of his cowboy boot dug into the dirt and spewed a shower of earth as he spun toward his horse.

Agamemnon waited patiently, tied to the back of the trailer. The blood bay gelding didn't shy at Buck's display of pique, just gave him a cool look as if to say, "Mother got the best of you again, huh?"

"I don't want to hear it, Aggie." Buck placed a hand on the gelding's rump as he stepped around him and into the trailer. He grabbed the padded horse blanket made espe-

cially for steer wrestlers and threw it on the bay's back.
"She cornered me. There was nothing I could do about it."

Get yourself hitched. That'll shake the loop out of her lasso.

Buck paused with his hands on the saddle as his grandfather's words drifted back to him. Buck's mother had been after him to marry some rich society girl ever since he'd come home with a master's degree in finance from the University of Pennsylvania's Wharton School of Business.

He'd escaped the same way he'd escaped his socialite parents' clutches since he was a boy—by going to the ranch his mother and father eschewed as beneath them. His grandfather, Bowen Buchanan, had been alive then and welcomed him, protected him.

Buck had earned his nickname on the Double Star by riding anything that couldn't stand a saddle. He'd lived in relative peace until five years after he graduated—when his grandfather died.

Since then, his mother's unrelenting pursuit of a "suitable" daughter-in-law had driven him from the ranch his grandfather left him. He'd gone rodeoing to escape. Most of the time she didn't know where he was or the unlisted number of his cell phone, so he had weeks of precious solitude.

Then, when he least expected it, she'd find him.

Get hitched. He rolled the idea around in his mind as he picked up his bulldogging saddle and settled it on Aggie's back.

Getting married would certainly foil any plans his mother had about foisting some debutante off on him. But hell, he'd been looking for a woman to love ever since he graduated. He sure didn't want a spoiled, rich, American princess whose only thoughts were of which parties she was invited to or the designer gowns she'd wear to them.

He wanted a woman who was as comfortable in a double-wide as she was on the back of a horse. A woman who didn't mind mucking out stalls.

A trailer-park queen. That's what he wanted. He'd always preferred women a little on the trashy side. But he wanted one with a brain, so she wouldn't bore him to death for the rest of his life.

He snorted. As if a woman like that existed.

Still, he considered the problem as he led Aggie toward Auburn, California's McCann Arena, which lay just beyond the lot where his trailer was parked among thirty-odd others.

Maybe he was going about this all wrong. He didn't necessarily need to be married forever—just long enough to convince his mother to lay off. Hell, he could pay some woman to marry him. Have her sign an ironclad prenuptial. A trailer-park queen would be grateful to earn as much money as he could afford to give her.

They'd get divorced after five or six months, and he'd have years to "recover" from his wife leaving him. Surely by then, he'd find a woman who'd make him happy.

Buck grinned. This sounded like a plan.

Now all he had to do was find himself a bride. The trashier, the better.

"Oooouuuuweeee! Will you look at that long, tall drink of sweet water?"

Buck tightened the cinch on Aggie, then turned to see what had his fellow steer wrestler so excited.

The sight of a young woman walking around the corner of one of the campers kicked him in the gut like his horse's hind leg. Leading a dun mare, she moved as if on the runway of the Miss America Pageant, though she was dressed in the gaudy starred-and-striped sequined weskit of the rodeo "court" and white jeans so tight he wouldn't be surprised if they'd been painted on.

As he watched, she paused and glanced around, then

twisted to tug at the seam riding up her rear end. The action was so sexy, Buck reacted as if she'd stripped right in front of him.

"Damn." He shifted his stance to ease the sudden tightness of his own jeans.

The other cowboy whistled. "I ain't never seen her around here before. Have you?"

"She must be that princess the rodeo director's been looking for." Buck stared at her through the chaos of horses, cowboys and cowgirls—a hunter whose crosshair was squarely on his quarry. "And maybe the one *I've* been looking for."

"What's that?"

"Nothing." Buck quickly wrapped off the cinch. "I'll go tell her they're waiting on her."

"Hey, I saw her first," the cowboy complained as Buck walked toward the young woman.

"Too bad." Buck threw a grin over his shoulder. "This little filly could be the answer to my prayers."

"Howdy, Princess."

The sound of her title made Josie's heart slam against her ribs even before she could untwist from her awkward position. She straightened to find a tall, broad, incredibly handsome cowboy smiling down at her. The sight as much as the panic at being found so quickly made her stammer. "What... How..."

With a smile that could melt the rock cliffs of Montclaire, he drawled, "They're looking for you."

Her eyes widened further. "For me? They are?"

Oh, no. How could they have found her already? Though it had taken an hour to ride across the fields toward the rodeo, she didn't think they'd even miss her by now. It was barely dark.

"Can't open a rodeo without all the princesses leading the procession."

She blinked hard. "*All* the princesses?"

"There are six of you, I think, not counting the queen." He pushed his hat back on his head. "Didn't you practice with the others?"

"Practice? No, I…" Josie dragged her gaze away from the cowboy's sexy blue eyes so she could think.

There weren't any queens or other princesses in California at the moment, that she knew of. These must be the beauty queens America was so fond of crowning. Melissa had said rodeos held a contest for a "queen" and her "court," but why would this cowboy think she was one of them?

A quick glance around the area told her. In the limited light, she could see three other young women wearing a sequined blouse identical to the one Josie had "borrowed."

Mon Dieu, I can't even steal properly.

After she'd cleared the fence that separated the Porter ranch from the rodeo property, she'd quickly realized her ball gown would stick out like a black sheep in a flock of white merinos.

Luckily—or so she'd thought at the time—these tortuous pants and the red-white-and-blue sequined blouse had been hanging on a trailer door at the edge of the lot. There'd even been a hat and boots to complete the outfit. She'd been desperate enough that it didn't take long to overcome her scruples about taking them. As she'd changed behind the trailer—one end of which bounced and squeaked rhythmically—she could hear loud moans coming from inside. She'd felt better then, thinking if the woman was sick she wouldn't need the clothes.

To help assuage her guilt, Josie left her own gown as payment. The Versace was worth at least ten outfits like the one she had on.

"You must be a substitute princess," the cowboy offered.

This was getting worse by the minute. If she claimed to be a substitute, she'd have to ride in the procession this man mentioned. She didn't think anyone would recognize her in this disguise, but she didn't want to waste any time. Soon either Madame Savoie or the bodyguards would realize she was missing. She wanted to have found a prospective husband and be long gone by the time they thought about searching the rodeo grounds.

But if she claimed she wasn't this rodeo princess, she'd have to admit stealing the clothes, which could put her in jail. Then Bonifay's men would locate her for sure.

Why couldn't she have found a plainer outfit to steal? One that would let her blend into the crowd?

"Are you okay, miss?"

She'd have to take her chances in the procession. Surely it couldn't take that long. The only problem was... "I don't know what to do."

He shrugged. "From what I can tell, it's not hard. Just ride around the arena with one of the sponsor flags. C'mon. I'll walk you to the gate."

Her eyes traveled uncertainly across the wide expanse of his shoulders. "But...who are you?"

His smile broadened, folding two deep dimples into his hard cheeks and stealing air from her lungs. He tipped his black hat. "Name's Buck Buchanan. Pleasure to meet you, Miss...?"

"Josie Fr—" She clamped her mouth shut to keep from uttering her French name. After a bare second's pause, she supplied the rough translation. "Freeheart. Josie Freeheart."

His dark brows moved together. "Freeheart? That some kind of hippie name or something?"

Not knowing how to answer, she lifted a shoulder. Freeheart sounded like a perfectly good American name to her.

To take his mind off her possible faux pas, she asked,

"Are you a rider of..." What did Melissa call those wild horses? "...broncs?"

"A bronc rider? Not anymore. But hey, we'd best get you to the gate. C'mon." He grabbed her hand and started walking toward the arena. "I'm a bulldogger these days. I used to ride broncs, but when you're six-two and two hundred twenty pounds, there's too much of you to be jerked around."

Josie barely heard his explanation. Her mind was so consumed with the sensation of her hand in his, she barely remembered to keep hold of her horse's reins.

Never in her life had a man held her hand. Not like this, palm against palm, fingers laced. The most she'd ever experienced was a man's hand wrapped around her gloved fingers as they danced. She'd never felt the heat that not only engulfed her hand, but shot up her arm to spread all over her body. Her heart began to race like it had when she escaped across the—

"Josie?"

"Hmm?" As she tried to shake off the curious sensation, she took one more step than he did, which landed her smack up against his side. The mare's nose shoved into her back, pinning her there.

Startled, she glanced up into eyes the deep blue color of the Mediterranean water surrounding her island home.

His smile made her heart beat even faster. "Meet me here after I ride, okay? I'll buy you a dog and a beer."

"A *dog?*"

He gave her an odd look. "Yeah. A hot dog."

"A hot dog. Oh."

What should she say? What should she do? None of the etiquette rules drilled into her at boarding school covered an invitation for *dogs* and beer.

Then she smiled. Of course they didn't. There weren't

any rules covering such a situation for a princess, because princesses didn't get into situations like this.

She was blazing new ground for princesses everywhere. She was on her own, free to do anything she wanted.

"A hot dog and beer sound wonderful."

Suddenly he dipped his head and pressed his lips against hers.

Shocked, Josie stiffened, her gasp cut off by virtue of no air. Only a second passed, however, before the lack of oxygen didn't matter. The only thing that mattered was that the contact go on forever.

She whimpered and pressed closer.

After a long, delightful moment, he drew away. "Damn."

She opened her eyes. His were so close she could barely focus on them. "You kissed me."

"Yep. I'm about to do it again."

"You are? Why?"

He chuckled. "For luck... among other things."

"Luck?"

"To help me catch my steer. The way I feel right now, though, I can't imagine not setting a record, just so I can get back to you."

The heart that had begun to slow began racing again. "All right. You may kiss me again."

The blue of his eyes darkened a shade, but he closed them a second before his mouth covered hers. His lips were warm and pliant, soft and—

Suddenly the point of physical contact lost focus as heat forged a bond that melded them together. Warmth flowed from him into her, then surged back again. The effervescence of it made Josie dizzy. To keep from falling, she grabbed his thick, hard biceps as his arms encircled her waist.

"There she is! About time. Tear yourself away from lover boy, Candy, or we'll start without you."

The rodeo director's words penetrated the sensual fog clouding Buck's mind, and he reluctantly drew away from the lips that had instantly sent him into a tailspin. He didn't want to stop kissing the trailer-park queen he'd just found. Not now. Not ever.

Slowly, she opened her fathomless amber eyes. He was gratified to note the trouble she had focusing, though the evidence of her desire made it hard not to bend and taste her again.

"Josie?"

"Hmmmm?" she asked dreamily.

This could be the stupidest thing he'd ever done, but he had a strong feeling it was fate slapping him up the side of the head. Why else would she appear so quickly, right after he'd made his plan?

"To hell with the hot dog. Will you marry me?"

Chapter Two

Josie's eyes widened and she pulled away, but only slightly. Then she gave him a nervous smile. "Yes."

"Candy, will you come on?"

She glanced at the rodeo director, who stood in a wide two-point stance several feet away.

"Hey, you're not Candy."

Buck ignored the man as he studied Josie's lovely face. Her black eyebrows and dark complexion told him she wasn't a real blonde, but that didn't bother him. Few trailer-park queens were. What made him hesitate was that she'd agreed to marry him so quickly, without asking a single question about his health or background.

Was it possible she knew he was Hardin Winford Buchanan II, son of the third richest man in Sacramento and multimillionaire in his own right?

He shook off the notion. He'd done his damnedest to keep his background secret from the rodeo world. More likely she figured he asked every girl he met to kiss him and marry him for luck. Cowboys did have a reputation for being superstitious.

"You don't think I'm serious," he said.

"Are you?" she returned.

"What the hell's going on here, Buck?" the rodeo director demanded. "What's happened to Candy?"

"One second, Hal." Buck's gaze never left Josie's intense amber eyes. "I have a few conditions."

She smiled wryly. "So do I."

"We'll talk about it on the way to Reno. It's just a couple of hours away, and we can get married tonight, if we haven't changed our minds by the time we get there."

She nodded. "All right. I'd like to leave as soon as possible."

Buck nodded, then turned to face the rodeo director, who watched them with a disgusted expression. "Sorry, Hal. This here's Josie. She's Candy's substitute."

"What? Where's Candy?" The tall, gaunt man held his palms toward them. "Never mind. I don't want to know. As long as I got someone to carry the Dodge flag, I don't care. Mount up, Josie. It's show time."

Buck glanced down at Josie, who stood in the circle of his arm. "You ready?"

She took a deep breath. "I guess so."

She guided the reins over the mare's neck as she moved down its side to mount.

Unable to resist the opportunity, Buck set his hands on her hips and lifted her onto the saddle. She was tall and though slender, she was no featherweight. Not that lifting her was any effort for him. Like most steer wrestlers, he was a big man, and he liked the solid feel of her.

With one hand on her knee, he grabbed her hands with his other as she gathered the reins. "Meet me here after I ride, okay?"

She sat ramrod straight in the saddle and looked down at him like a princess from her throne. Her golden-brown eyes searched his face as if he were an animal she'd never seen before. "Will you kiss me again...for luck?"

The contrast of her haughty posture and provocative words made desire stab deep into his gut. "Better not, sweetheart. I might not be able to stop. But I'll definitely take you up on that offer later. Hell, if we're getting married, we're going to be doing a lot more than kissing."

Crimson brushed across her cheeks, but the smile she gave him was as brilliant as the arena lights. "I'll meet you here."

He released her, and with a gentle kick, she sent the mare toward the gate where Hal was waving her on frantically.

Buck pushed back his hat and watched her pause to lift the Dodge Truck flag, then maneuver into place beside another princess, who watched her curiously.

Will you kiss me again?

Was it possible he'd finally found a woman who didn't feel the need to play games? One who was unafraid to match his libido kiss for kiss, caress for caress, thrust for thrust?

And to top it off, she was beautiful, sexy and a trashy trailer-park queen to boot.

Okay, not a queen, just a princess, but that would do.

He hoped like hell his instincts were right. If they were, he couldn't wait to take her home tomorrow night to meet the folks.

With a smug smile, Buck turned back toward his horse.

His mother was going to have a heifer.

"Four-point-six seconds!" the announcer bellowed over the loudspeaker. The sound carried easily to where Josie hid among the trucks and trailers. "The best bulldogging time of the evening, folks. Buck Buchanan rode like a man possessed! Let's give him a great big hand. He's in the money tonight."

Dieu merci, he was fin—

No. *Thank God* he was finished. If her charade was going to be successful, she had to weed the French words from her vocabulary. *Thank God* her English was unaccented and full of American slang and idioms, courtesy of all the years she'd known Melissa.

Josie peered around the cab of a truck, but couldn't see Buck approaching. She hoped he hadn't changed his mind.

She needed to get away, fast.

After sending the mare she'd borrowed back over the fence toward the Porter stables, she'd spotted a young woman carrying the Versace gown. Despite a red flush on her cheeks and neck, the woman didn't look sick at all. In fact, she was obviously angry and looking for her stolen clothes.

Then a local sheriff's car pulled up at the edge of the parking lot. When two deputies began showing the people milling around a picture, Josie had to assume they were looking for her.

So far she'd avoided being found by either Candy or the cops. But what would she do if Buck Buchanan didn't show up? What if he'd changed his—

Her attention was snagged by the swaggering gait of a tall, muscular man leading a horse from the arena. Though he was silhouetted by the bright lights, she knew it was Buck.

More than relief flowed through her. As she remembered how his big, hard body had felt against hers, how his lips had nearly caused her to spontaneously combust, her heart began pounding like the drums that had welcomed her on her state visit to Kenya. The sensation distracted her so much she didn't realize he was looking for her until he called her name.

"Sssshhhh!"

Buck peered into the shadows on the parking lot and saw a piquant face surrounded by enormous blond hair peeking around the cab of a truck. Relief flooded through him. "What are you—"

"Come here." She waved him over. "Hurry, please."

Her impatience made him recall the desire biting at him ever since they'd parted. He grinned as he joined her behind the truck. "Want another kiss, sweetheart? Well, here I come—ready, willing and more than able."

She grabbed his arm and hauled him into her hiding place, glancing nervously behind him as she did. "Can we leave now, please?"

A little miffed that she hadn't wanted the embrace he'd been craving for over an hour, he pushed his hat back. "I reckon. What did you do with your mare?"

She glanced over her shoulder. "Oh. I had to give her back. She wasn't mine."

He nodded. Borrowing mounts at rodeos was as common as muddy jeans from dirt landings. Still, he had the feeling something wasn't altogether what it should be. Josie didn't act like a woman excited about getting hitched. She didn't seem excited at all. She seemed distracted, worried...almost scared.

He cussed as the most likely possibility hit him. "You running away from something, sweetheart?"

Her only answer was to look away guiltily.

Damn. He knew his trailer-park queen was too good to be true. "What is it? The law? Or am I going to have a jealous husband breathing down my neck any minute?"

She was clearly horrified. "Would I be marrying you if I was already married?"

He shrugged. "It's not legal, but it's been done."

She shook her head vehemently, which made her blond hair slip a bit to the side, enough to release a dark lock of hair.

Buck smiled. A wig. Who wore wigs but old women and trailer-park queens?

She really *was* the kind of woman he was looking for.

"Nothing like that, I promise," she insisted. "It's…my father. He wants me to marry a man I don't want to marry. I have to get away from here as soon as possible. Please help me."

Her obvious anxiety and the fact that she didn't evade the question made Buck believe her. Or maybe it was because his own parents were trying to do the same thing to him.

He drew a finger across the satin smoothness of her jaw. "I bet the guy's rich, isn't he?"

She nodded solemnly. "Will you help me? Please? I don't have any money at the moment, but I do have a couple of pieces of jewelry I can sell that should bring enough money to pay you."

"Pay me?" Buck chuckled at the ridiculous notion. At least it proved she didn't know who he was. Relieved she wasn't a gold digger planning to alimony him out of his money, he slipped his free hand around her back and bent to kiss her temple. "That's cute, sweetheart. Of course I'll help you, but you don't have to pay me."

She craned her neck so she could see him. "Yes, I do. You'll understand more when I tell you what my conditions are. But please, can we talk about them on the way to Reno?"

"I just have one question. How old are you?"

She looked puzzled, but answered, "I'll be twenty-five in three weeks. Why?"

"You're legal. Good. Just checking." He gathered his gelding's reins closer. "You have any suitcases?"

She shook her head.

Hell, she really was running away. "Let me load Agamemnon and pick up my check, then we'll head on out."

"If you'll show me where your trailer is, I'll load your gelding while you pick up the check. It'll be faster."

His gaze swept her worried face. "Someone's here right now, looking for you, aren't they?"

She hesitated, then nodded.

"Hell, my check's not that big. We'll just go ahead and—"

"No." She placed a hand on his arm. "You need your check. Melis— Um, I know how rodeo cowboys live."

He wasn't going to tell her that he always signed his rodeo checks over to the next charity he came across. His only stipulation was that the donation remain anonymous. He didn't want to let his rodeo buddies know he needed these checks about as much as the Double Star needed hills.

"All right." He pointed out his red Chevrolet truck attached to a two-horse trailer with a built-in camper. Both were battered, with chipped paint. He'd spent several days making them look that way. Inside they weren't fancy, but both held all the basic comforts a man or horse could want. "There's my rig. It's not locked."

She nodded and moved her hands to Aggie's reins. She stroked the horse's nose as she let him nuzzle her hand to smell her scent, then she moved to each side of the gelding so he could see her out of both eyes. "Sounds like you performed well tonight. You deserve a good rubdown."

The evidence that she knew and respected horses made Buck's admiration rise even more. He brushed his mouth against hers. "I'll be back in ten minutes."

Even if he had to hound the rodeo secretary to sign his check.

"Isn't that wig uncomfortable?"

Startled by Buck's question, Josie turned from the side mirror where she'd been watching for vehicles that might be following them. They'd left Auburn twenty minutes ago, heading into the mountains toward the Nevada state line.

Up to now, Buck had been quiet, intent on guiding his rig onto the I80.

"Wig?" She had a moment of panic, having been convinced she'd had everyone fooled.

For an answer, he reached across and tugged at a strand of dark hair lying on her cheek. He pulled until the long tress was free from beneath the wig. "You're not a blonde."

Her stomach fluttered at the way he was caressing the black strand, and she drew it from the masculine fingers. "Does that matter?"

"Not at all." He sent a glance down her form. "It just makes me wonder what else isn't real."

Since he was eyeing her overly generous bust, she sighed. He might as well know the worst now. First she eased the wig off her head. She couldn't suppress a moan of relief when the pressure of the tight band holding it in place was gone.

Strands of hair escaped her once-perfect chignon, but she couldn't make any repairs at the moment other than pushing them off her face. Then, casting an uneasy glance at Buck, she reached inside the sequined weskit and began pulling tissues from the bodice.

When he saw what she was doing, Buck smiled, then chuckled. The next time he glanced over, he started laughing out loud. The more tissues she took out, the harder he laughed.

When she was finally finished, she glared at him.

He looked at her, and kept laughing.

A smile tugged at Josie's lips, and when she glanced down at the mountain of tissues on her lap, she let her lips curve.

"Is there anything left of you in there?" he asked, wiping at tears of mirth.

Josie held the weskit against her bust. "Not all that much, I'm afraid. I guess it was false advertising, but I needed a disguise. If you want to back out of the deal, I'll understand.''

"No, I definitely want in."

His voice had such a husky quality, she glanced at him. The hot looks he was sending her between glances at the highway surprised her. She'd caught looks of unbridled lust on men before, but never directed at her. No man had been so lacking in manners as to openly desire Princess Joséphene of Montclaire. It just wasn't done.

Until now.

A wave of heat washed through her, but not from embarrassment. For the first time in her life, she felt like a woman—a sexy woman. She'd had no idea that being the object of a man's desire would feel so wonderful, so liberating, so wanton.

"You—" She had to clear her throat before she could speak properly. "You still want to get married?"

His gaze rested on hers, then shifted back to the highway. "Do you?"

"I…" She turned her own gaze to the line of headlights coming at them. "As I said, I have some very specific conditions."

"Such as?"

"Well—please don't take this personally—I only need a husband for a few months. But at least you won't be stuck with me for long."

Buck glanced at her sharply. "A few months? Why?"

"I…I'd rather not go into the specifics. Suffice it to say that I need to prevent my…father from marrying me to someone else."

Buck was amazed at how her situation was like his own. "How many months are we talking about?"

She shrugged. "I don't know exactly. At least two. Perhaps as many as six or seven. It depends on how long it takes me to—''

She cut herself off so quickly, he had to probe. "To what?"

"To...make other arrangements."

"What other arrangements?"

"Does it matter?"

"If I'm going to be involved in this, yes, it does."

She cleared her throat. "All right, then. I have to find a husband. A real husband, I mean. One who...meets certain qualifications."

"Which I lack."

"Please don't take this personally."

Buck frowned when he realized that he wasn't particularly insulted. What he didn't like was the thought of Josie marrying someone else. He didn't like it one bit. He felt almost...possessive, which didn't make any sense. He'd only known her a few hours.

Then a possibility he liked even less occurred to him. "So you're wanting a marriage in name only."

"No," she said quickly. "I...it needs to be consummated. That is, if you don't mind."

Mind? Hell, if no sex had been one of her conditions, he'd have put her out at the next town. She'd had him so aroused from the instant he laid eyes on her, he was having trouble convincing himself not to pull the truck off at the next exit and down the first dark road so he could have her right now. He'd never be able to keep his hands off her for a couple of months.

"No." He shifted in the seat. "I don't mind."

She sighed, as if she'd been worried about it. "Good."

"Any more conditions?" he asked.

"Just one."

"And that would be?"

"We need to have a prenuptial agreement. Not that I don't trust you, but—"

"You don't know me."

"Exactly. You don't mind?"

"A prenuptial saying that what's mine is mine and what's yours is yours, and we don't get a nickel of each other's money or assets, such as they are." He smiled. "Sweetheart, the only assets I can see that you have are what God gave you."

"I have enough to pay you five thousand dollars for your help." She sounded a bit offended.

Buck chuckled. Five thousand dollars. He'd been prepared to offer her fifty times that to marry him for a few months. Should he tell her? No. Let her think he was doing her a favor. However... "I'm not taking a dime of your money, Josie. So put that thought right out of your pretty head."

"But—"

"I don't need it. I don't want it. I'm not taking it."

"If you're certain..."

"Absolutely. Any more conditions?"

"No." She sighed. "I guess that's that, then, isn't it?"

"I guess so."

"We're getting married?"

"I'm game if you are."

"Didn't you have some conditions?"

"Not anymore, sweetheart."

The purr of the engine as the car ran the dark highway was the only sound for several seconds. Then Josie said, "I like it when you call me that."

"Sweetheart?"

"Yes."

Her soft confession touched him. He reached across the cab to capture her hand. "No one's ever called you sweetheart before?"

"No."

"Good." He laced his fingers through hers. "C'mon over here."

He dragged her across the bench seat, against his side.

He was on the way to Reno to marry a beautiful, sexy trailer-park princess. He couldn't wait to see his mother's face when he walked into his house tomorrow.

Yep. The next few months were going to be very interesting.

He felt as if his whole body was smiling.

"I now pronounce you man and wife."

Josie froze, staring at the bald justice of the peace through the filmy veil, the only part of the bridal costume she wore.

Wife.

Mon Dieu. What have I done?

She'd married a total stranger for the sake of Montclaire. A man she'd known only a few hours.

With the help of a penlight from his glove compartment, she'd scribbled a brief prenuptial, which they'd both signed, with the justice of the peace and his wife as witnesses. But a prenuptial wouldn't protect her from any vice he might have a tendency toward. She didn't know anything about this man.

Was her country worth such a personal sacrifice?

The justice cleared his throat. "You may kiss the bride."

"Finally," Buck murmured.

Josie allowed him to turn her in his arms.

He fought a moment with the veil. "Why the hell did I insist you wear this thing?"

Finally, he cleared a path to her face. His gaze searched hers for a long moment, probing, hunting—for what, she didn't know. Then he smiled. "I told you I'd kiss you again."

His lips touched hers, and all thoughts of Montclaire flew right out of her head.

Josie woke to the soft sounds of birds chirping and waves lapping gently at a shoreline. Accustomed to hearing the ocean only when a rough storm passed over the Mediterranean, she opened her eyes to find herself curled up in a narrow bed sandwiched between a metal wall and a cabinet with a tiny sink.

Sitting abruptly, she noticed how restrictive her clothes were and glanced down. The stars and stripes of the sequined top gleamed dully in the sunlight trying to break through the tiny blinds on the tiny windows. The sight of the stolen clothes brought everything back.

She swept her left hand in front of her face. A plain gold band purchased at the Reno wedding chapel circled her ring finger.

She was married. To a cowboy.

Panic and relief hit her simultaneously, so hard she couldn't breathe. She was on her own, with no bodyguards, no royal trappings, nothing familiar to protect her.

On her own. Though it had called her like a siren song since she was a girl, the concept was foreign to Josie. She'd never, ever been truly on her own. Not one single moment of her life.

But she was now. Since she'd used the English version of her name on the wedding certificate, no one knew she was Princess Joséphene of Montclaire. She could do anything she wanted, act any way she wanted, be anyone she wanted.

Smiling with a euphoric sense of freedom, Josie fell back onto the pillow, only to discover that the tiny bed wasn't quite long enough for her five-foot-nine-inch frame.

"Ow."

She rubbed her head. This must be the camper built onto the front of Buck's horse trailer. He must have carried her in here after she'd fallen asleep in the truck. She hadn't meant to go to sleep, but she'd had an exhausting week.

Josie wondered vaguely where she was. Lake Tahoe?

That's where Buck said they were heading when they left the chapel. He knew of a campground on the shore of the lake that had special spaces for campers with horses.

Not that it mattered where she was. She was free. There was no way Bonifay could trace her on the road with Buck Buchanan.

No, not Buck. What was the name he'd put on the wedding certificate?

Hardin Winford Buchanan.

He'd given her a hard look when he gave the court clerk his name, as if he expected her to make fun of it. She'd squeezed his arm to reassure him. Who was she—Princess Joséphene Eugénie Béatrix Marguerite Isabeau Francoeur— to make fun of such a name?

Buck fit him better, just like Josie fit her.

She craned her neck to peer around the camper.

Speaking of Buck, where was he? Why weren't they in the same bed? She'd always had the impression that middle-class American couples slept together.

She glanced at the floor, then a movement higher caught her eye. Two large, bare feet poked out from a sheet on the other side of the trailer.

He must have put her to bed, not wanting to disturb her sleep with husbandly demands.

A smile drifted across her face. He might be just a cowboy, but her husband had the manners of the finest gentlemen she'd ever met.

Not that she would have minded being disturbed. As a matter of fact, they needed to proceed with the consummation as soon as possible.

Heat stung her cheeks, and she sighed. She wished they'd accomplished it last night, so she wouldn't have to worry about it. Now, how was she going to bring it up?

Perhaps she wouldn't have to. Perhaps Buck would take matters in hand.

She giggled at the unintentional pun. His hands had seemed more than capable of taking care of matters last night.

But his caresses and kisses weren't the only reason she liked him. They'd talked all the way into Reno. He seemed fascinated by everything she'd said, just as she'd been with the details he revealed about his life.

What felt so good, however, was knowing his fascination wasn't because she was a princess. To him, she was an ordinary woman.

How often had she longed to be just an ordinary woman? To meet a man who would see beyond the brilliance of her crown to the woman beneath?

She frowned as she realized Buck didn't know she had a crown. She wasn't being honest with him, but she couldn't risk it. Not yet. Not until she was certain what kind of man she was dealing with.

When she didn't surface after a few days, her face would be splashed over every newspaper and television in America. Bonifay would offer a reward—a large one.

Melissa had told her that most rodeo contestants lived from paycheck to paycheck. From what she'd seen so far, she didn't think Buck was the kind of man to be seduced by money. He'd refused her offer of payment, after all. But she'd only known him a few hours.

She still couldn't believe she'd married a perfect stranger. Yet there was something about Buck that she'd trusted immediately. Though she couldn't pinpoint a reason for her trust, somehow she was certain he wouldn't harm her. When she first looked into his deep blue eyes, it was as if she'd known him all her life.

Was it because his eyes reminded her of the ocean surrounding Montclaire? Was it because his height and build reminded her of her father? Was it the way she felt when he'd kissed her after they'd said ''I do''?

Remembering that moment, she closed her eyes to savor the things he made her feel—even hours after the contact. The scent of a hardworking man blending with the scent of a hardworking horse—she couldn't imagine anything sexier. The caress of his warm breath on her cheek, the way his lips molded to hers.

She moaned softly as she traced her fingers over her lips.

"You okay, sweetheart?"

Her eyes flew open to see Buck sitting up on the elevated bed.

Her breath caught.

Bent slightly because his head and long torso wouldn't fit in the cramped space, he yawned and reached a muscular, naked arm up to scratch his shaggy, dark brown hair. But his arm wasn't all that was naked. Every part of him that she could see was nude—from the wide, well-defined expanse of his chest to the strong legs ending in long, high-arched feet.

Only his hips were covered. A sheet appeared to be all that lay between her gaze and his most private parts.

The warmth she'd been feeling at the memory of his kiss intensified, especially when she realized she wanted to snatch the sheet away so she could see all of him.

Never in her life had she experienced desire so sharp it felt like raw, aching need. Desire to see a naked man.

But not just any naked man. This one.

Her passion was so unfamiliar and acute, it alarmed her. Princesses didn't have feelings like this.

Josie's mind caught on her words.

Princesses might not have feelings like this, but ordinary women did—and that's what she was until she returned to Montclaire. She knew she'd have to go home eventually, but until then she wasn't going to have any more *princess* thoughts. She was going to enjoy every single, solitary minute of being an ordinary woman. The memory of these few weeks would have to last the rest of her life.

"You look kinda flushed, sweetheart. You too hot?" he asked.

Josie gave in to the need to giggle, something Joséphene would've suppressed. If only he knew how hot—and why. "I'm...fine."

He gave her a puzzled look, then started to slide down to the narrow sliver of floor below him. As the sheet began to slide off his hips, however, he stopped. "Maybe you'd better use the bathroom first."

She would much rather have enjoyed the show, but since he didn't seem inclined to give her one, she realized she was in dire need of facilities. That there were any nearby surprised her. "There's a bathroom in here?"

He pointed to the wall behind her. "You'll have to fold up your bunk so you can open the door. I don't have the water hooked up for a shower yet. It was late when we pulled in. But there should be enough in the tanks to flush a few times."

Josie placed her feet on the floor and took a moment to stretch. "Where are we? Lake Tahoe?"

He rubbed a hand over his morning beard. "Yep."

With a nod acknowledging the information, she stood and turned to fold the bed. She stared at it for a moment, then pulled the top sheet back—he hadn't bothered with a bottom one. Uncovered, the hinges were obvious. After a minute of bending and stretching, she'd reconfigured the bed into a small couch.

Satisfied with her job, she straightened and turned to smile at Buck. The look she caught on his face trapped the air in her lungs. His eyes were like the hot blue centers of twin flames, and they were burning into her bottom.

She suddenly realized the view she'd given him, bent

over in the tight jeans. He would have been able to see every curve of her form.

A shiver ran through her—part excitement, part fear.

He wanted her.

A few men had told her they wanted her, but she hadn't really believed them. Perhaps because none had looked at her like this. They couldn't separate the woman from the princess. She could see it in their eyes.

Buck's own eyes rose slowly to hers, losing none of their heat during the languorous journey.

Mesmerized, Josie stared straight into the face of desire. His need inflamed her own, which excited her and frightened her even more.

"Josie, sweetheart?" he asked in a deeper, huskier voice than she remembered him having.

"Yes?" The word was hesitant, breathless.

"Either go into the bathroom, or climb up here and let's get on with what we're both wanting to do."

Josie didn't follow either suggestion. The fire burning through her veins had welded her feet to the floor.

She wanted to climb up next to him more than she wanted to see Montclaire again—ever. She wanted to run her hands over the relief map of his chest, to dig her fingers into the thick mane of dark brown hair, to press her mouth to his well-defined lips.

Then she remembered. She could. In fact, she *should*.

She took one hesitant step toward him. "We *are* married."

She didn't think his gaze could heat up any more, but he proved her wrong. The closer she went, the hotter his gaze grew. Finally she stood at the base of the chest-high bed, feeling as if she were burning alive.

One strong hand gently pushed back a lock of the hair that she vaguely realized was falling in wisps around her face. He glanced somewhere over her shoulder, closed his eyes as if in pain, then cussed and drew back his hand.

"We can't," he groaned.

"Oh. I…" Her face flaming from her rejected brazenness, Josie spun away.

Buck grabbed her arm. "Where are you going?"

Too embarrassed even to face him, she waved somewhere in the direction of the bathroom.

"Look at me."

She couldn't.

"Sweetheart, look at me."

She turned slowly until his fingers caught her chin and forced her to look at him. "If we make love now, I won't want to stop. Probably for days. It's already noon and—I'm extremely sorry to say—we've got to attend a party tonight. We've got to stop somewhere along the way and get you a dress to wear. As lovely as that outfit is, it isn't appropriate for the party."

Panic raced through her. "Party?"

"Yeah. My mother conned me into it."

Josie relaxed, picturing a kindly older woman, as oblivious of Montclaire's existence as her son. "But I don't have money for a dress."

He smiled. "Don't worry, sweetheart. You're my wife now. I'll buy whatever you need."

She shook her head and dug into her jeans pocket. "I can't allow you to do that. We're only going to be married a few months." She held out a pair of earrings. "I have these to sell. They're probably worth several thousand dollars."

Certain they were fake, Buck barely glanced at the earrings she dropped into his hand. She was so cute, thinking her costume jewelry was worth thousands of dollars. He decided not to burst her bubble. He would tell her he pawned them, then give her the money she expected.

"Can we stop at a place where I can sell them?" she asked.

He shrugged. "Let me take care of it."

She sighed. "I don't know how to thank you. You've helped me so—"

"Hush now." Bending, he slid a finger under her chin and lifted her mouth to his. "One kiss, sweetheart. Then *go*."

Chapter Three

"A princess!"

Buck snatched the newspaper from the counter of the gas station where he was getting the truck filled.

No. This couldn't be true.

But the woman in the photo, staring stony-eyed back at him, looked exactly like Josie. Her hair was twisted up in a much more elaborate do than the one she'd taken down before they drove into Carson City, and instead of a Resistol, she was wearing a tiara.

A damned tiara.

The caption beneath the photo claimed this was Princess Joséphene Francoeur of Montclaire.

Joséphene. Josie. Josephine, she'd spelled for the court clerk last night. No coincidence. His wife was a princess. A real, honest-to-God, crown-wearing, kiss-her-hand princess.

"Princess Joséphene Missing; Feared Kidnapped," the headline screamed.

Buck scanned the article that told how she'd attended an

American friend's wedding at the Porter ranch outside Auburn, California. The horse she'd evidently slipped away on had returned to the stable, riderless. The article went on to speculate about rumors that had been flying through the press about her imminent wedding to Alphonse Picquet, one of the richest men in Europe. By press time no one had an explanation for her disappearance, but the police were not ruling out foul play.

Foul play. Buck barked out a mirthless laugh. The only foul play had been committed by the princess herself—by conning him into marrying her.

Princess.

He threw the paper down as if it had suddenly been smeared with an offensive substance.

What the hell did she think she was doing? And why the hell had she chosen him as her scapegoat?

His eyes narrowed. Did his mother have something to do with this?

He shook his head. As much as Alicia Buchanan wished she hobnobbed with royalty, he knew damned well she didn't.

She wasn't going to, either. There was no way he was taking Josie to his father's party tonight. His mother would be drooling so much they'd have to bring in buckets just to catch it all.

A damn princess. Not of some major European country, but—

Wait a minute. Royalty married royalty, didn't they?

His mouth twisted in derision. Obviously not.

Alphonse Picquet certainly wasn't royalty. He was a shipping tycoon whose greedy fingers reached all over the world. Buck had felt the strength of those fingers in an investment he'd made a couple of years back. Picquet had tried to play dirty. Only Buck's quick influx of cash had saved the deal.

The guy was Eurotrash. He was more than twice Josie's age, with all the charm and attraction of a bull moose. And if the rumors were true, his sexual appetites tended toward the bizarre and sometimes violent. The little princess had evidently heard about the women Picquet had scarred—mentally and physically—so she'd conned Buck into marrying her instead. But that was understandable—smart of her, really. It was the other....

Rage threatened to blind him. Fury at her deception.

She'd said she was looking for a husband with "certain qualifications." She must be trying to find someone as rich as Picquet, but not quite so perverted. Someone like...

Hardin Winford Buchanan II.

And he'd fallen for her act—bridle, saddle and reins. Hell, he'd aided and abetted her.

Buck's bout of cursing was cut off by the gas station attendant opening the dirty glass door. "You're not quite a quart low. Want me to top her off?"

Buck pulled his mind back with an effort, then nodded. "Forty weight."

The teenager ducked inside for a can of oil, then lumbered back out to Buck's truck, his head moving like a goose.

Buck followed him outside. Standing in the heat, Buck's gaze wandered up the street to the mall on the outskirts of Carson City where he'd let Josie out to shop while he supposedly pawned her earrings.

Now he remembered how she'd pulled her hat low on her brow as she'd stepped down from his truck. Probably to keep people from getting a good look at her face. Probably because she knew her face would be splashed across newspapers all over the country. Hell, all over the world.

"You're ready to go," the attendant announced.

Buck handed over enough cash to cover his bill plus a tip, then climbed in and cranked up the truck. But he didn't pull out. Instead, he stared up the street toward the mall.

He'd thought he knew what Josie was after, but he couldn't forget the real fear he'd seen in her eyes. He had just enough doubt to make him hesitate.

She really hadn't seemed to know who he was, and she'd offered to pay him to marry her.

But why marry him in the first place? Why an interim husband? She seemed pretty desperate to get married quickly. Why not just refuse to marry Picquet?

Hell, he didn't know.

Maybe she was after his money, or maybe she just thought cowboys were too dumb to read a newspaper.

Either way, he didn't like it.

He reached into his breast pocket for the diamond earrings she'd entrusted to him that morning. Now that he had a good look at them, he knew her assessment of them was accurate. They were worth several thousand dollars. Hell, their true worth was probably triple that, seeing as who owned them. People paid big money for gewgaws owned by royalty.

He remembered how he'd planned on giving her several thousand dollars for the diamonds he thought were fake. He'd wanted his trailer-park queen to have nice clothes for once in her life.

Hell, Princess Joséphene probably shopped at the most expensive couturiers in Paris. He wondered if she'd bribed the missing rodeo princess for her sequins or if she'd stolen them.

Stolen, probably. She hadn't exactly been flashing her princess card around.

He rolled the earrings around in his hand, a bitter smile creeping across his face as a plan formed. Whatever her reasons for choosing him for whatever scheme she had in mind, she'd picked the wrong cowboy.

So she wanted to be his little trailer-park queen for a few

months, did she? Fine. That's exactly how he was going to treat her.

Princess Joséphene Francoeur of Montclaire was about to get a taste of how the other half lived. He didn't think she'd like living in the real world. In fact, he'd make damn sure she didn't.

He threw the earrings into the glove compartment. He'd keep them as a souvenir. Then he pulled into traffic, betting she'd scream "Manicurist!" the first time she chipped a nail.

Josie noticed the sudden quiet in the shop and glanced over to see the two salesladies' attention riveted outside. Following their gaze, she smiled. Buck stood on the other side of the mall corridor, waiting for a break in the cross traffic.

Tall, with broad shoulders and narrow hips, he stood ramrod straight, as if king of all he surveyed. When he moved, it was with a casual grace one didn't expect in such a large man. He looked as if he'd be at home anywhere—on a ranch, at an elegant party....

On a throne.

No.

Josie spun back to the racks she'd been inspecting.

She couldn't think like that. She'd go crazy if she did.

So she was attracted to Buck. So she went weak in the knees when he kissed her. It was just because he was a nice man. She'd probably feel the same way about any man who helped her escape marriage to Picquet.

It was only the heady rush of freedom. An understandable response to the incredibly intimate sensations of a man's lips on hers, his warm hand resting on her hip, his fingers playing with her hair.

That's all it *could* be. She couldn't let herself fall in love with a poor cowboy. If she did, she wouldn't be satisfied with any other man, and she had to marry a rich husband—for Montclaire's sake.

It would be better if she could take the money from the earrings and say "Thank you, but goodbye" to Buck. If he wasn't around, she couldn't fall in love with him.

But she couldn't leave—not until they consummated the marriage.

"Find anything?" he asked when he reached her side seconds later.

She shrugged. "Not really."

"Just as well," he told her. "You won't need a fancy dress, after all. The party plans have been canceled."

She melted in relief. "I see. Why don't you just take me to Wal-Mart, then?"

He blinked. "Wal-Mart? You'd rather go to *Wal-Mart?*"

She didn't know why he was looking at her so incredulously. He didn't know she was a princess. Besides, she'd always bought a few pair of Wranglers when she was visiting Melissa. She preferred wearing them because they were designed for working on and around horses.

"All I need are some jeans and a few shirts. And some..." Josie felt color creep under her skin. But an ordinary woman would be able to mention intimate apparel to her husband, wouldn't she? Still, she had to clear her throat before she could say, "Undergarments."

His eyes seemed to catch fire even at the euphemism. His gaze burned into hers for an endless moment, before he shook his head and collected himself. "Well, that's good. 'Cause I got some good news and some bad news."

Though distracted by his reaction to her simple need, Josie froze. News. Had her disappearance been discovered soon enough for it to make today's newspapers? "What?"

"Well, the bad news is your diamond earrings are fake. The guy at the pawnshop was only going to give me ten bucks for them."

"Ten dollars!" The salesladies she'd refused help from earlier threw surprised looks her way, so Josie lowered her voice and shifted so her hat blocked her face. "Those earrings were worth more than ten dollars. Much more."

"You're right. That's the good news." Buck reached into his shirt pocket. "I took them down to a jeweler, and he gave me fifty."

He handed over the money proudly, as if he'd done her a great service.

Josie stared at the bills he held out, her heart sinking several stories below her feet. What was she going to do now? She'd been counting on living off that money until it was time to return to Montclaire. Because she couldn't find the pack of clothes and money Melissa had hidden in the tack room, the only thing else she had to sell was the necklace Melissa had given all her bridesmaids.

But since Melissa had also given Josie the matching earrings as maid of honor, the necklace was probably fake, too. They were all the jewelry she'd worn to the wedding, because she hadn't wanted to outshine the bride.

She didn't understand. Melissa's father could afford to buy first quality diamonds for every woman who'd attended the wedding. And Melissa was not one to scrimp on presents, especially not to Josie.

All she could conclude was that her friend had been cheated.

Josie felt cheated, as well.

"Don't worry, sweetheart." Buck slipped an arm around her shoulders. "It'll all work out."

"How?" she whispered. "I was counting on the money from those earrings to see me through until...until after we divorced."

"I'm your husband now, sweetheart. I'll—"

"No! This isn't a real marriage."

His dark brow raised. "I thought you said it was."

Heat crept into her cheeks. "Well, yes, in some ways it is, but we're not planning on staying together long. We're not going to…to fall in love or anything. It's not fair for you to pay my expenses."

He rubbed his chin. "Tell you what. How about you work for room and board? Help out around the place. Cooking. Cleaning. Taking care of Aggie. That kind of thing."

Josie lowered her gaze, giving herself time to sort through the emotions flooding through her at his kind offer.

She didn't mind working. She was used to helping care for a stable full of horses. And although her cooking abilities weren't extensive, she could prepare basic meals—thanks to the headmistress of the exclusive British boarding school. The practical, steel-spined woman had insisted that every girl learn to cook, no matter how many servants she had.

What worried Josie was this crazy attraction. If she was around Buck twenty-four hours a day—working with him, sleeping with him, relying on him for everything—how would she prevent herself from falling in love with him? That the word *love* occurred to her at all told her she was already halfway there, after just a few kisses.

She lowered her gaze until it slashed across the broad expanse of his chest. She knew exactly what he looked like under the worn chambray shirt—how his sculpted his chest was, how flat his stomach, how straight his shoul—

Mon Dieu. The sex was only going to make it worse.

Her gaze ran back up the line of snaps to Buck's face. His blue eyes bored into hers, the heat in them stealing her breath.

On the other hand, what choice did she have? With no money, she'd have to find some way to live or go back to Montclaire and allow Bonifay to annul this marriage so she could marry Picquet.

"Your offer is very kind, but—to be frank—what reward would you receive from the arrangement?"

For the briefest instant, desire burned across his face like wildfire. He quickly quenched the flames, however. Squaring his shoulders, he gave her a hard smile. "Someone to cook my eggs every morning."

"I'm not exactly a world-class chef," she admitted.

He shrugged. "You've got to be a hell of a lot better than me. I usually live on fast food."

"Dogs and beer?" she asked, deliberately reminding him of how they'd gotten themselves into this mess.

His face softened, and he reached for a strand of hair, then abruptly dropped his hand. "Sometimes. Besides, Grandpa's soul would possess Aggie long enough to make him give me a hard kick in the rear if I were to leave a lady stranded."

Though he hadn't spelled it out, Josie knew he wanted her. And she wanted him. If she fell in love, she'd just have to deal with that when she left. She'd have to suppress her personal feelings for the sake of Montclaire.

Which shouldn't be hard. She'd had a lifetime of practice.

"All right." She hardly recognized her voice through the huskiness. "For the next few months, I'm your employee." She smiled. "And wife."

His head began to dip toward hers, but he checked himself. He straightened and cleared his throat. "You ready to go?"

Josie looked down at the money she couldn't remember taking from his hand. "This isn't enough to buy much, even at Wal-Mart."

He paused, then said, "I passed a secondhand store down the street. You wanna try that?"

Josie smiled. A princess wearing secondhand clothes. Her father would have a stroke. "Sounds like fun. Although I don't want to get secondhand...um, undergarments. Can we stop for those at Wal-Mart?"

He gave her an odd look, then shook it off. "For you, sweetheart, anything."

Buck stood at the end of the Wal-Mart checkout counter, watching Josie pay for the package of cheap cotton panties she'd selected. The young woman checking her out kept looking at her curiously, and he fought a smile as he watched Josie try to keep the brim of her hat between her face and the clerk's eyes.

"You sure do look familiar," the young woman finally said.

Josie shrugged. "I'm told that a lot."

"That'll be seven-twenty-nine. You been in here before? I swear I know your face."

Josie didn't reply, just handed over a ten-dollar bill.

The clerk thoughtfully punched in the amount. As the cash drawer popped open, she spun back to Josie with a gasp. "You're that princess that's been missing. Your hair's down and you don't have makeup on, that's why I didn't recognize you right off."

Josie went as still as doe sensing danger. "Princess?"

"Bless my soul! Marge, come here, quick! We've got the Missing Princess here at Wal-Mart!"

"Yeah, and I'm the Queen of England," Marge said in a bored voice from the next counter. "Can't you see I'm busy, Brenda?"

Josie seemed to shrink into her hat. "Believe me, I'm no princess."

"They say you were kidnap—" Brenda gasped and threw a horrified glance in Buck's direction.

Knowing he had to save Josie or risk going to jail for a crime that hadn't even been committed, he chuckled loudly. "Princess?" He moved to slide a hand around Josie's waist. "The closest my ol' lady's ever been to royalty was vying for rodeo queen—and she didn't even win that."

The clerk glanced from one to the other skeptically. "You sure are a dead ringer. There was a picture in the paper just this morning."

He gave Josie a peck on the cheek. "Hear that? Sounds like you've got a future as a princess look-alike. You could make us rich."

Josie smiled nervously. "I'll stick to horses, thank you."

The clerk finally gave up with a sheepish grin. "Yeah, I guess you're right. They say everybody's got a double. And how many princesses shop at Wal-Mart in Carson City, Nevada? Oh, well. Here's your change. Two dollars and seventy-one cents. Thanks for shopping at Wal-Mart. Come again."

"Thank you." Josie took the money and the package, then pulled Buck down the short aisle and out of the store.

"What's your hurry, sweetheart?" He didn't bother to hide the derision in his voice and face. "Afraid somebody's really gonna think you're the princess?"

"Sure. I hate all that bowing and hand-kissing. It's so embarrassing." Her attempt at mockery might have worked if he hadn't known better.

"We'd better get Your Majesty back to the castle, then, so you can rustle up some grub. Your prince is starving."

She finally relaxed and gave him a genuine smile as he unlocked the truck. "If my prince wants something decent to eat, he'd better buy some groceries. The only thing you have in your cabinets is a can of tuna."

He opened the door for her to climb in. She threw her package onto the stack of clothes she'd picked out without incident at the secondhand store, then climbed in. She still wore the white jeans, though she'd borrowed one of his T-shirts to replace the sequins.

The sight of her tight bottom wiggling into place made heat flash through him without warning.

He stiffened. How could he still want her after what she'd done?

She was a damn princess. A debutante times ten. He'd never wanted a debutante in his life. He sure as hell didn't want a princess.

"Oh, prince?"

He glanced up into her playful eyes and for some stupid reason felt glad the fear had left their amber depths.

Damn.

"What?" he barked.

She frowned. "Are you all right?"

"Yeah." He closed the door, barely restraining himself from slamming it. He walked around and climbed in behind the steering wheel. "We'll pick up a couple of burgers on the way out of town."

She shrugged. "You're the boss."

Yeah, he was.

Buck shoved the keys into the ignition and started the engine.

If only he didn't have to keep reminding his libido of that fact.

Two hours later, Josie heard the truck backing into their camping site and hurried outside to make sure Aggie wasn't in the way. She'd taken him out of the small corral on the opposite side of the area so he could graze around the trailer.

Eyeing the groceries in the back of the truck, she grabbed the gelding that was on his way to be stroked by his owner and led him back into the corral as Buck climbed down.

"Only three bags?" she called. "You couldn't possibly have gotten everything on my list."

He snorted. "Like Carson City, Nevada, ever heard of a Portabella mushroom. And what the hell are capers?"

"If the grocery store in Auburn has them, Carson City

would.'' Her eyes narrowed. ''You didn't even look for them, did you?''

''Hell, no.'' He leaned on the tailgate and pushed his hat back. ''I stuck with the three basic food groups—steak, beans and beer. If you're going to complain, next time I'll make you go.''

His words effectively shut her up.

To avoid another incident like the one at Wal-Mart, after they'd brought the hamburgers back and eaten them, she'd insisted Buck do the grocery shopping by himself. She used washing her new clothes as an excuse to stay at the camp-ground.

As she moved next to him to take one of the bags, he leaned toward her, as if about to kiss her. She lifted her face in anticipation, but he stopped himself with a muttered curse and grabbed a couple of bags instead.

Frowning, Josie pulled the remaining bag from the truck. Why didn't he kiss her? She wanted him to. It didn't seem right that he hadn't. She was his wife, after all.

Following him into the camper, she began putting the groceries away. True enough, about all she found was steak, beans and beer. The only other items were milk, bread, eggs, bacon, coffee and soft drinks. Plus several jars of jalapeño peppers.

What was she going to do now? She didn't even have the ingredients for a basic roux.

Buck pulled the last cold soft drink from the tiny refrig-erator and sat down on the tiny couch. His huge frame dwarfed the cushions that had made up her bed the night before.

Recalling the way he'd reacted that morning to the sight of her bending over, she deliberately put as many things as she could in the lower cabinets. She wanted to punish him for not following her grocery list—and for not kissing her.

Her strategy seemed to work for several minutes. His tortured eyes followed every movement she made.

Suddenly he drained the last of the soft drink from the can, then released a loud belch.

Josie started and whirled to face him.

He grinned unapologetically and crushed the can in his large hand.

His actions were so blatantly male, so shamelessly primitive, Josie couldn't hide a smile. He was like a stallion showing off his prowess for a mare.

She'd never had her very own *human* stallion.

Her amusement, however, seemed to irritate him. Scowling, he reached into the last bag and drew out a newspaper. With a sharp flick of his wrists, he snapped it open and buried himself behind it.

Confused and a little miffed by his contradictory behavior, she started to turn back to the groceries when her attention was snagged by a photo on the front page of the newspaper.

Her photo.

Chapter Four

Josie's eyes widened, and her breath caught in her flash-frozen throat.

Had Buck seen it? Was this his subtle way of telling her he knew who she was? Was that why he was acting this way?

She had to know.

Slowly setting down the jar of jalapeño peppers on the counter, she stepped over and raised the newspaper so she could see the photo. It was the official one released by Montclaire, taken just before her twenty-first birthday when she'd been officially instated as the heir to the throne. She wore a gown with a pearl-encrusted bodice, with a sash across it in the blue, green and yellow colors of Montclaire, held in place by her official badge of office. On her head was her mother's diamond tiara.

"Did you see this?" she asked softly.

He flipped the newspaper back. "What?"

"This." She pointed to the picture. "It must be the princess they were talking about."

"Oh, that. Yeah, I saw it." He seemed uninterested, and went back to the article inside.

Josie couldn't let herself feel relieved until she had a more definitive answer. "Do you think I look like her?"

Buck's blue gaze roved over her face, then moved back to the photo. "Not really. This dame looks like she's got a cattle prod stuck up her butt. I bet she's never set foot in a camper, much less cooked supper in one. Hell, she's probably never cooked, period. And I bet she's never, ever bought panties at Wal-Mart. A fabric other than silk would probably give her a rash. Why? You saying you're her?"

She tried to give a convincingly derisive chuckle. "Right. Princesses hitch rides with cowboys all the time."

"You're two entirely different women, believe me. Hadn't you better get those groceries put away? Be time to start supper soon."

He flipped the paper back open, dismissing her.

Josie returned to her task, but she was unable to forget his words.

You're two entirely different women.

He didn't know how accurately he'd hit the target. She'd always been two entirely different women—a princess, and the woman inside who just wanted to be like everyone else.

She remembered when that photo was taken. She'd *felt* as if she had a cattle prod up her butt—put there by the photographer and all the makeup and wardrobe people fussing over her.

She didn't feel that way now, though. She'd never felt so relaxed in her life, so free. She felt just as she did when she worked in the stables on Montclaire, only now she knew it would last longer than a few hours, because she didn't have some onerous princess duty to hurry back to.

Yes, she'd been working hard all day. Not only had she hand-washed all her "new" clothes in the camper's tiny sink, Buck had told her to scrub down the horse trailer while he was gone. It was good, honest work, though, and she enjoyed doing it.

She wished this time could stretch into forever. But it wouldn't. She only had a few weeks before she'd have to return to being a princess.

Zut. No, no. She meant *damn.*

Josie took a swallow of her soft drink, then leaned back in the folding lawn chaise with a sigh of relief. It was the first time she'd sat down all day.

She tipped her chin up to catch the breeze that wafted off the crystal-blue waters of Lake Tahoe. Dusk was falling all around her. A small, plump bird with a black cap hunted energetically for insects in the pine trees towering over her, calling out his success with a three-note whistle.

She'd never had a day like today. Except for the little scare at Wal-Mart, she'd spent the entire day just like an ordinary woman—shopping, cooking, washing clothes, working beside her man.

All right, so Buck was just her man for a little while. She could pretend, couldn't she, that this would last forever? After all, she was pretending she wasn't a princess.

If only she had some hope of spending the night like an ordinary woman. But Buck had been a perfect gentleman all afternoon.

It was if he'd suddenly turned off a switch. Before she'd agreed to stay with him, he'd acted as if he wanted nothing more than to toss her into bed and have his way with her.

A delicious shiver ran across her skin. Then she opened one eye and frowned at the trailer.

Ever since the incident at Wal-Mart, however, he'd acted more like a boss than a lover. Not that she'd ever had a lover or a boss, other than Bonifay. But Buck acted just like the prime minister ordering the servants about—telling her to scrub down the horse trailer while he drove into town for the groceries.

Buck had done the heavy chores when he returned, lifting out the grain sack to feed Aggie and moving the picnic table closer to the camper so they could eat on it. Ever since supper, he'd been locked in the camper, "working."

She didn't know what a roving cowboy had to work on inside a camper, but she wasn't exactly an expert on cowboys, so she didn't say anything. Now she was enjoying the solitude—a rare commodity for her on Montclaire—and wondering how a princess could seduce a cowboy.

It's not that she didn't know anything about sex. After all, she'd been breeding horses ever since she was a girl. But from what she'd experienced so far, the human mating ritual was vastly different. Mares didn't lose control of their thinking apparatus when stallions were close by. The stallions were the ones that went bonkers.

She sighed. Knowing the mechanics of sex and knowing how to seduce a man were two entirely different things.

The only thing that had worked so far was the sight of her bottom in the tight jeans. What was she supposed to do, stick her tail in the air every time she wanted Buck to kiss her?

She giggled at the image that sprang to mind, but her mirth was cut short by a hot, heavy, wet tongue swiping across her face.

Josie's eyes flew open and her hands came up to defend herself. As she saw the culprit, however, she chuckled and reached up to rub the muzzle the gelding had stuck through the corral. "You're nothing but a big old pet. Spoiled rotten, that's what you are. Only work a few seconds a couple of times a week. Pretty good life for a horse, if you ask my opinion."

Buck quietly stepped out of the camper in time to see Aggie's unashamed demand for affection. He watched as

Josie cooed to the gelding and ran her hand over his large head, and suddenly realized he was jealous of his horse.

Damn.

He'd kept his hands and his lips to himself all afternoon, which had only served to make him frustrated and surly. Staying away from Josie felt unnatural.

Realizing that made him even surlier.

Hell, he'd only known the woman twenty-four hours. How could she have already insinuated herself into his life so completely that he felt a wrench when they were apart? It had been all he could do to keep his mind on buying groceries when he was in town earlier. All he'd wanted to do was return to the camper, to kiss her, to touch her, to make sure she was still there.

Damn. Damn. Damn.

She was a princess, for God's sake. A princess in need of a rich forever-type husband—and she might just have him in her sights.

Even though she didn't seem to know who he was now, that didn't mean she wouldn't figure it out. She was one smart cookie, and even if she hadn't married him for his money, once she discovered he had more than enough to qualify as her husband, she sure as hell wouldn't let him go without a fight.

He had to admit she didn't act much like a princess, though, or even a debutante. When he'd ordered her to clean out the trailer, he'd been certain she'd refuse. When she hadn't, he'd been certain she wouldn't have completed the chore by the time he got back.

Not only had she made Aggie's trailer shine from top to bottom, she'd washed all her new clothes and had them hanging on a line she'd rigged from the camper to a tree. When he'd seen her white cotton panties flapping in the breeze and realized they were the high-cut French kind that bared a woman's hip for a man's touch, he'd nearly lost every shred of control he'd been desperately hanging on to.

Now here she was, making goo-goo noises at his horse.

If he hadn't seen her picture in the paper that morning and on several sites on the Internet during the last hour, he'd never have believed she was a princess.

The evidence, however, was irrefutable.

Damn her lying little soul.

Stepping down, Buck moved over to push Aggie's head back into the corral. If Buck couldn't have any loving from Josie, his horse could damn well do without it, too. "Come on, you old son-of-a-gun. You're bothering the lady."

"He's fine," Josie protested, though she leaned back in the chair. "I'd ask how he got so spoiled, but I'm pretty sure I know."

"Yeah?" He pushed Aggie away, then hauled out the other lounge chair that had come in the set and unfolded it next to her. "How?"

She grinned. "You. You're a big marshmallow. I've seen how you pet him when you think nobody's looking."

Her smile caught his attention. He'd spent the past hour on his laptop computer, finding everything he could on the Internet about Princess Joséphene of Montclaire. Nearly every picture accompanying the articles was of an unsmiling young woman with haunted eyes. Not a single one had shown this relaxed, smiling beauty.

The realization that she was smiling for him caused light to flood into a part of him so deep he didn't know it was there, didn't know it had been dark.

Buck scanned her beautiful face in the twilight. Though it was a classic oval with regular, even features, the slight slant of her amber eyes and the fullness of her mouth gave her an elfin look. Especially when her smile was so impish. Hatless now, her black hair spilled around her shoulders, utterly straight, but thick and luxurious.

He wanted to bury his hands deep in the silky strands and use them to pull her playful lips closer, urging them to play with his. The knowledge that he had every right to touch her, that she was in fact expecting him to, felt like a knife twisting in his gut.

"Admit it," she said.

He turned his gaze to the lake, shoving the desire away just as he'd gotten rid of Aggie, only to discover that shoving the nine-hundred-pound horse was easier. To punish Josie, he decided to pick at her, to see how much she'd tell him about life as a princess. "How'd you learn so much about horses?"

She hesitated, then answered with a little too much nonchalance. "How does anybody learn? By being around them."

"So you have horses at home?"

She shrugged. "A few."

"Horses aren't exactly cheap animals to keep. In fact, they're a hell of an expense. How can a trailer-park queen afford 'a few'?"

"Trailer-park queen? What's a trailer-park queen?"

Buck cussed inwardly at the slip. He'd better be careful, or he'd reveal more about himself than he wanted to. But now he had to explain. "A woman who lives in a mobile home."

"I never said I lived in a mobile home."

He cussed again. No, she hadn't, now that he thought about it. He'd leaped to that conclusion himself when he saw her walking out from the trailers parked behind the rodeo. His libido again, making assumptions based on wishful thinking. "Where do you live?"

She shrugged. "I doubt you've heard of it."

"Try me."

"What about you?" Her voice was stronger now, on the attack instead of defensive. "How does a poor rodeo cowboy afford to keep a horse? Aggie is a quality mount. I doubt he was cheap.''

Touché. He really was going to have to watch himself. He'd always been attracted to smart women, especially if they dressed in tight jeans and came with a smart mouth. "Aggie earns his keep, and mine, too."

She folded her long legs up close to her. "Why the sudden inquisition?"

He thought about telling her straight out that he knew who she was, and that he wasn't going to fall for her trickery. It would be the smartest thing, he knew. The safest thing.

But it would also send her away, and the thought of her leaving made him want to rip down the nearest Jeffrey pine with his bare hands.

To avoid delving into the meaning behind that violent notion, he went back to his gentle attack. "I just wondered how you know so much about horses."

"How did *you* learn so much about horses?" she countered.

"I grew up on a ranch." Thinking he might get her to talk if he told her about himself, he told her about being raised by his grandfather on the California ranch northeast of Sacramento. Though he knew he was being as mendacious as she was, he left out the part where he kept running away from his parents' two-point-eight-million-dollar home, making his way to the Double Star any way he could, until his parents let him live on the ranch with his grandfather.

Josie discussed her motherless childhood, how she took comfort and found self-worth in raising horses.

Buck certainly understood that. He'd discovered at an early age that horses didn't give a damn how much money you had. They kicked you just as hard as they'd kick a poor man if you did something they didn't like.

They talked until the stars had all popped out, each giving

only the safest parts of the truth, and just enough of that to satisfy the other.

Only Buck was aware of how much was missing on both sides.

Still, the game intrigued him. *She* intrigued him.

Josie never actually lied, but there were several times when she danced around the truth so ingenuously, proving her intelligence, that he had to shift in the chair to hide his reaction from her.

At some point, he realized he'd taken her hand in his. He didn't know when and he wasn't going to speculate on why, but the connection felt natural, as if it linked two parts of a whole. Her skin against his felt good, too—though it made him long for more.

Her soft voice in the darkness, her quick mind, her clean, womanly scent had him tied in so many knots that when it came time for bed, he sent her in and stayed outside another hour, so he could be certain she was asleep.

He couldn't let his libido ruin his plans. He'd held out against marrying a woman like her for over ten years. There was no way he was going to give in now.

"Do all cowboys sleep like they're dead?" Josie murmured as she picked up the saltshaker she'd dropped on the floor of the camper.

Though she hadn't been quiet about making breakfast—chopping onions and peppers, and rattling pots and pans in a vain search for an omelet pan—Buck hadn't stirred a hair since she woke just before dawn. He was so still, in fact, she'd turned on the overhead light to make sure he was breathing.

She sighed as she carefully folded the omelet over on itself. At least she'd found enough ingredients to make a halfway decent breakfast. She was rather proud of her ingenuity, actually, considering her limited cooking abilities.

After cutting away the edges of some moldy cheese, she had enough to add body to the eggs. With the peppers Buck had been eating out of a jar like candy last night and the small onion she'd found hiding behind the sugar, she had a colorful and, hopefully, piquant breakfast to serve her husband.

Husband. The word held all sorts of possibilities—none of which she'd experienced. She frowned at the long, high-arched feet poking out from under the sheet two meters from her face.

She'd enjoyed their talk last night under the stars. She'd been breathless with anticipation, expecting Buck at any moment to lead her into the trailer and make love to her. But when she could no longer keep her eyes open, exhausted by all the physical work that day, she'd come into the trailer alone, undressed alone and gone to bed alone.

She'd been tempted to crawl onto the mattress Buck occupied now, which extended back into the gooseneck portion of the trailer. But when the time actually came, she didn't have the nerve to be so brazen. Instead, she'd folded out the bed she'd found herself in that morning—half nervous, half hoping Buck would wake her when he came in and insist she share his bed. He hadn't.

Josie stared blindly down at the omelet, which sizzled softly.

What was wrong with her? Why wouldn't Buck make love to her? Was she so ugly? She thought he wanted her. She saw something in his eyes that looked like desire. But ever since they'd gone into town yesterday, he'd acted as if they were platonic roommates, not husband and wife.

Zut. Damn. What was she going to do? She needed to consummate this marriage. They could be discovered any day. The future of her country was at stake.

She glanced at Buck again, and had to admit Montclaire wasn't the only thing on her mind. She wanted her husband with a deep, gnawing ache—which surprised her enormously. The few men she'd dated had been sophisticated, charming, wealthy men of the world. That was the kind of man she'd always expected to marry—though Alphonse Picquet only met one of those requirements.

Now that she thought about it, however, she hadn't been especially attracted to any of those men. Certainly none of them had made her feel like this—breathless, weak in the knees, yearning for a smile, willing to commit who knew what kind of crime for a kiss.

What did this say about her—that she was attracted to a poor cowboy who probably wouldn't know a shrimp fork from a salad fork? Whose idea of complimenting a meal was a loud belch? Who knew more about manure than the stock market?

Josie frowned as she slid the omelet onto a plate.

It probably wasn't anything to worry about. She was attracted to him, no doubt, because she associated him with the freedom she was experiencing, not because she loved him.

No, definitely not because of love.

She couldn't possibly love a man like Buck. There was no way she could stay married to him, so loving him would only cause her pain.

Josie set the plate on the table, then turned to wake her husband. What she needed to do was keep things light. Make their short time together fun. As soon as she got serious, she was afraid her heart would, too.

With that in mind, she stepped over to the bed and lightly stroked a fingernail up one long foot, then down the other.

Buck twitched his toes, then wiggled his feet.

Josie smiled, then yanked one of his toes.

"What the—?" He sat up too quickly, knocking his head on the low ceiling of the trailer.

Josie laughed. "You *are* alive!"

He rubbed his head and glared at her. "What's that supposed to mean?"

"That you've been sleeping as soundly as a body in a coffin."

Josie looked so damn beautiful standing there, all regal even in secondhand jeans and T-shirt, that Buck had to force his gaze to the clock so he wouldn't reach for her. "Eight-twenty. Damn, I'm getting lazy."

"I guess having a slave is exhausting, isn't it?" She gave him an arch smile.

He wasn't about to justify all the work he'd had her do yesterday, because he planned to give her even more today. He'd worked her so hard she'd been sound asleep when he finally came to bed last night—which was exactly the way he'd planned it.

It had been hard enough to crawl into bed alone, wanting her as much as he did. It had been even harder to fall asleep, knowing she was just six feet away, knowing she was more than willing to satisfy his hunger. That's why he'd slept so late today.

She sighed and swept an arm toward the table. "Breakfast is ready, master."

"Did you feed Aggie this morning?" He wrapped the sheet around his waist and scooted off the bed.

"Yes, master."

"You can drop the sarcasm."

She giggled. "Yes, master."

He glared at her but didn't say anything as he stepped into the bathroom to dress. When he came out, she was seated at the table. She looked comfortable sitting there, like he'd always pictured his wife would. Before his mind could send the correct interpretation of the picture she made, his body reacted.

To keep her from noticing, he pointed at the yellow blob on the serving plate. "What's this?"

He knew perfectly well what it was, but he felt like giving her as hard a time as she was giving him. That she didn't know she was giving him a hard time made his mood even worse, because it made him feel petty.

Her surprise was obvious. "An omelet."

The look she gave him was so incredulous, he said, "No, just a cowboy."

She blinked. "Pardon me?"

"You were wondering if you were talking to a moron." He slid into the bench seat across from her. "No. Just a cowboy."

"I thought everyone knew what an omelet was."

"From now on, just fry up three or four eggs along with some bacon and toast. That's fancy enough for me. Okay?"

"Sorry." She reached for the plate and started scooting out of her seat.

He placed a hand over hers. "This'll do for today, since you've already messed up the eggs."

She lifted a brow. "We can always give it to Aggie."

The omelet looked so delicious, he wasn't about to let Aggie have one bite. "Sweetheart, if this green stuff in here is those jalapeños, Aggie wouldn't touch it with a ten-foot pole."

She glanced worriedly at the omelet. "Is there something wrong with the peppers?"

"Not for humans." He narrowed his eyes at her. "You haven't tried them?"

She shook her head.

He picked up his fork and cut off a bite of the omelet, then held it across the table. "Open."

She obediently opened her mouth. He slid the bite inside.

She chewed several seconds, then made a sudden choking sound. Her black eyes grew wide and two bright red spots popped out on her cheeks.

He *almost* felt sorry for her. The princess manners no

doubt drilled into her at an early age kept her in the chair for another whole minute, though he swore he could seem steam rising from her ears. She even tried chewing some more, which only made it worse.

Finally, she couldn't stand it any longer. But instead of spitting the bite out onto her plate or even into her napkin, she rose daintily from the table, then ran into the bathroom.

Buck released the laughter he'd been struggling to hold in. He guffawed so hard, it ate up some of the sexual energy that had been building to a bursting point inside of him.

Bless her, she was more entertaining than a slew of drunk cowhands on a Saturday night.

Chapter Five

"How'd you like me to point out a few constellations?" Buck asked that night into the quiet darkness. "Can't see much of the sky because of the trees, but I think..."

He trailed off as he glanced at Josie. They'd turned off all the lights to enjoy the stars, and he could barely see her in the moonless night. "What I think is that you're asleep."

He squeezed the hand he'd been holding. Taking her hand was an unconscious act, and he never could remember exactly when he reached for it.

The fingers entwined with his stayed limp.

He frowned. He'd driven her hard all day, trying to make her crack—but she wouldn't. In fact, she seemed to enjoy the work he gave her. He'd actually heard her singing, for God's sake.

He could still feel the tremors that had shaken him when he'd heard her low-pitched voice singing a French song he didn't recognize.

Damn, he wanted her. Every minute of the day, every second of the night he wanted nothing more than to bury himself deep in her tall, trim, sexy body.

He wanted her now. He was getting hard just thinking about it.

Damn.

He shifted on the lawn chair. Knowing she was his wife and more than willing didn't make it any easier. He knew he could gently shake her awake, pull her onto his lap and do anything—

No, he couldn't.

Beside the fact that she was exhausted was the very definite fact that he didn't want to be stuck with a damn princess.

Although he had to admit she didn't act very much like a princess. There were moments when her regal upbringing showed, but most of the time she acted just like any ordinary woman.

She sang while she worked. She talked to Aggie as she groomed him. She rolled up her jeans to wade in the lake. She cooked and cleaned and decorated the trailer with wildflowers.

And she seemed to love every minute of it.

He found that sexier than anything. He'd been looking for a woman who was as comfortable in a double-wide as she was at one of his mother's society dinners. A woman who didn't mind mucking out stalls. Who wouldn't feel out of place walking down the aisle of Bergdorf's or down a dirt road. Who was part beauty queen, part trailer-park queen.

The woman he wanted was lying in the lawn chaise beside him.

Buck stood so suddenly he ripped his hand away from Josie's, causing her to murmur a complaint and shift on the chair.

He stopped, willing her to return to the depths of sleep. He sure didn't need her waking now. No telling what he might do.

Josie settled, and in a moment her breathing once again became shallow and regular.

When Buck realized he was staring at the way the starlight cast shadows on her lovely face, he cussed and strode over to the lake.

Aggie nickered from the corral, but Buck ignored him.

Gazing blindly over the star-dappled water, he tried to corral his thoughts.

Josie was *not* the woman he'd been looking for all his life. She was the exact opposite. What he was looking for was a trailer-park queen with a little class, not a real queen who might not mind getting her hands dirty every now and then. There was a huge difference between the two.

He was not going to sleep with Josie. No how. No way. He had to keep his jeans zipped, no matter how tight they got.

Aggie nickered again, and Buck turned around. He groaned when he realized he still had to put his wife to bed.

"Here we are."

Buck pulled to a stop in front of the launderette, pleased with himself for having thought of this little job for Josie. After two days of throwing every dirty rotten chore he could at her, he hadn't elicited one single complaint, much less sent her scurrying home. But she would hate the tedium of doing laundry. Everyone did.

Josie eyed the place with a frown. It fit right into a part of town that had seen better days. Paint was chipping off the concrete-block exterior, and duct tape outlined the cracks in the glass that made up the front wall. "Why couldn't I just wash your clothes in the sink like I did mine?"

"Because it's more than clothes. We've got sheets and towels here. They're too big for any sink, much less the one in the camper. And my jeans need the agitation of a washing machine to pound out the dirt I grind into them every time I haul down a steer. In fact, you'll need to run them through the washer a couple of times to get them clean.''

"If the sink's too small, I can always use the horse trough.''

He caught himself before he laughed. He didn't want to let Josie know how much he liked her smart mouth. It might encourage her, and then where would he be? "C'mon. You're the wife, and this is women's work.''

"Wife? Humph. Not yet, I'm not,'' she muttered as he shoved open the door.

Knowing she was talking about their nonexistent sex life, he ignored her sarcasm and stepped down from the truck. After lifting four stuffed pillowcases from the bed, he strode into the launderette.

Fortunately, Josie hadn't come right out and asked for sex. It was fortunate because he didn't know what he'd do if she did. He was hard-pressed now to keep his hands off her, with her polite attempts at seduction. If she got down and dirty, he'd be a goner.

Josie took a full minute to follow him. She poked her head inside the door, looked around, then entered.

He knew what she was doing—making sure there was no one here who'd recognize her. He'd thought of that. Since it was midmorning on a weekday, no one else was here.

He tossed the clothes on top of two washing machines and pulled ten ones from his wallet. "Here, this should be enough. I'll be back in a couple of hours.''

"What? Where are you going?''

"I've got to go see about getting a nail out of one of my tires.''

"Oh.'' She stared around as if she'd never seen such a place in her life.

He'd bet twenty-to-one she hadn't. "You *do* know how

to do laundry, don't you? Any idiot could work these machines.''

"Oh." Her frown deepened. "Sure."

"Good. Then I'll be back in about a couple of hours. Two and a half at the most."

"Two hours?" She grabbed his sleeve. "But...but..."

He had to steel himself against the panic in her huge, amber eyes. He was doing this for her own good. She didn't belong with him. "But what?"

"What if I need you?"

The word *need* pierced him. He suddenly realized he wanted her to need him. He wanted to be the one she turned to when life got rough, the one who could make her big, bad world go away.

But he had enough trouble making his own big, bad world go away. No. He had to be hard-hearted—for both their sakes.

"Need me for what?"

Her gaze darted about, obviously searching desperately for some reason to keep him there.

He peeled her fingers from his arm. "Go on, now. I need to get to the service station."

Buck walked out of the launderette, callously ignoring the forlorn expression on his wife's face. He fully expected to return in a few hours to find her in tears, begging to go home to Prince Daddy. He didn't care if his jeans were shrunk to toddler size or his underwear was blue. He could afford new clothes.

What he couldn't afford was to have Josie around long enough to break down his resistance. If he consummated their marriage, he'd be stuck with a princess for the rest of his life. And he wanted a princess for a wife about as much as he wanted to marry a Longhorn heifer.

When the tire repair took only forty-five minutes, he drove around, which gave him too much time to think.

Leaving her like he did made him feel like a jerk. He couldn't forget the panic on her beautiful face, and he soon became concerned.

What if someone came into the launderette and recognized her? What would she do? Run away to avoid capture? What if she ran and he couldn't find her?

A little over an hour after he left, Buck found himself pulling up to the corner across the street from the launderette. Someone else was in there now, because a well-preserved late-eighties Chevrolet was parked in front.

Buck strained to see through the front wall of windows, but the reflections of the traffic going by hindered his sight. He thought he saw two figures moving around inside, but he couldn't tell if one of them was Josie.

After worrying about her for several minutes, he couldn't stand it any longer. He had to know. If Josie had bolted, there was no time to lose.

He pulled into the parking space next to the Chevrolet, then rushed inside.

She stood at a table in the back, helping an old man fold towels. She laughed at something the man said, then replied in a voice drowned out by the dryers churning their loads.

Buck's eyes narrowed, and he shoved his hat back on his head.

She was having a good time! While he'd driven around, worried sick about her, she was in here having a damn party with some old man.

The guy must've said something about him, because Josie threw a worried glance over her shoulder. She smiled when she saw him and waved, relief clear on her face because he wasn't someone who could give away her identity.

Since he was caught, Buck sauntered back to where they were working. "How's it going, sweetheart?"

He even bent to give her a peck on the mouth, just to

make it perfectly clear to the old man whose woman she was.

Josie's expression showed surprise, but she recovered quickly, her princess manners taking over. "Just fine. Buck, this is Mr. Ludlow. Mr. Ludlow, this is my husband, Buck Buchanan."

Mr. Ludlow reached a hand across the stacks of towels. "Howdy."

Buck shook his hand firmly. "Nice to meet you."

"Mr. Ludlow came in just after you left," Josie told him. "He and I have been talking."

"I can see that. Our clothes about done?"

She cast a questioning glance at Mr. Ludlow, who shrugged. "The shirts might be, but you just put them jeans in the dryer. And they're gonna take at least another fifty-cents worth."

Obviously the talking going on had been Josie talking Mr. Ludlow into showing her how to do laundry. Sneaky little princess.

The trouble was, Buck admired her cleverness and her courage for reaching out to someone who might have recognized her. He felt almost...proud of her.

Damn. Things weren't going according to plan. Not at all.

Josie smiled when she heard Buck's truck rumbling down the campground road the next morning. She'd only been with this man five days, and she already recognized the sound of his truck.

Obviously Aggie knew it, too, because the gelding ambled over to the side of the corral nearest the spot where Buck parked.

Josie rose from the lawn chaise she'd retreated to after mucking out Aggie's open air "stall." It was a back-wrenching job, but better than going to the grocery store with Buck and risking recognition. Since the storage facilities in the trailer were minuscule, trips to the store were necessary several times a week.

She stopped to wait by the picnic table, fluffing the wildflowers she'd arranged that morning in a tomato can. She'd used the tomatoes in the chili she'd cooked the night before.

Josie's smile widened. When Buck had demanded the dish for supper, she'd panicked. The only chili she'd ever eaten had been at Melissa's, and she'd never, ever considered making it.

Luckily, she'd found a recipe on the side of the ground chili pepper. Even if she said so herself, it didn't turn out half-bad.

Buck backed the truck in and climbed down.

"Did you get *anything* on the list I gave you?" she asked with little hope.

"What list?" he asked with a grin.

She shook her head and reached for a bag in the bed of the truck. "I wish you'd let me make what I'm good at. Then you'd really get a nice meal."

"You haven't done half-bad." He stopped her with a hand on her arm. "I'll carry the groceries in."

She laughed and stepped away to give him room.

He strung his arms through all six of the plastic bags and lifted them out of the truck. "What's so funny?"

She crinkled her nose at him. "Just the fact that you think nothing of having me lift thirty pounds of manure on a rake, but you won't let me carry in a bag of groceries."

He scowled. "You can open the door."

"Yes, master."

He growled his displeasure at her sarcasm, but didn't say anything.

She preceded him into the trailer and stood aside as he placed the bags on the table. Then she reached into the nearest one to begin putting the food away.

To her surprise, Buck lifted a six-pack of soft drinks out of a bag and put them in the small refrigerator. When he stood and caught the amazement on her face, he demanded, "What?"

She shook herself and stepped over to place two cans of beans into a cabinet. "Nothing."

For the next few minutes, they worked together silently, putting away the groceries. Josie enjoyed the companionship. This must be what married life was really like for ordinary people. She was going to miss this kind of thing when—

Just as she bent to place a bag of potatoes in a lower cabinet, Buck turned to put a sack of sugar in a top cabinet, ramming his crotch against her upturned bottom.

They froze.

Even through their jeans she could feel him grow hard. And bigger. And even harder.

He swore under his breath—the sound strained, choked. But he didn't pull away.

She felt as if she'd never be able to breathe again.

Was it her imagination, or did he press into her even more, rubbing himself ever so slightly against her?

She dropped the potatoes with a thud.

Her heart pounded like storm waves against the shores of Montclaire, rushing blood to her head, making her dizzy. Her mouth went so dry, she could barely whisper, "Buck?"

His hand ran down her hip. "Hmmm?"

She straightened and twisted so she could see him without breaking the contact. "Buck, please—"

That's all she managed because as soon as her lips were within reach, his mouth descended. At the same time, his arms came around her from behind, and he ground his hips into her bottom.

They groaned in unison.

Josie had never felt such mind-numbing heat. It seared

through her body to her brain, burning away rational thought, leaving little but raw, aching need. And what she needed was to feel him against the part of her that was throbbing.

She wrenched around in his arms so she was pressed to him—lips to lips, chest to chest, hips to hips. Immediately, she felt a rush of hot, wet heat. She moaned into his mouth and rubbed herself against him.

Buck grabbed the back of her thighs and lifted her. He splayed her legs around him and placed her on the edge of the cabinet.

She locked her ankles around his hips, driving him closer. She dug her hands into his hair, thrusting his hat off. It must have dropped to the floor, but she couldn't hear it hit over their moans.

His mouth left hers and burned a trail across her cheek. He breathed her name into her ear and bit her lobe, breaking the tentative hold she had on her ability to think.

She was a writhing mass of desire—aching, wanting, needing nothing but his hands kneading her breasts, his tongue sliding against hers, his hot skin under her fingers.

To open even more territory for her questing hands, she grabbed the edges of his shirt and yanked. The snaps gave with a satisfying rip. She dug her fingers in the light mat of hair, dragging her nails over the planes of his chest.

"Josie. Damn."

"What?" she murmured.

"No."

"Yes."

He groaned and ground himself against her even as he said, "I can't."

She grabbed handfuls of his shirt. "Please, Buck. I want you. I need you. Please."

"No. I can't."

"It's all right," she whispered. "We're married."

He tore himself away from her so violently she fell off the cabinet. Staggering, she caught herself on the sink.

"Why are you—" His voice was thick, strained, choked. "I can't. Damn you. I can't."

"Buck..."

"No!" He shoved the trailer open and rushed out.

Josie's confused mind registered the sound of Aggie's whinny, then an engine roaring to life. Gears ground into place, then gravel pinged against the side of the trailer as tires spun away.

Just like that, Buck was gone.

Two hours later, Buck pulled the truck into the parking space.

Having spent the rest of the morning pondering what had happened, Josie didn't turn from her task of feeding Aggie.

She wasn't stupid. It was obvious he'd wanted her, but for some reason he was determined not to make love to her. She couldn't imagine what his reason could be, unless he'd thought better of having sex with a wife who was only going to be around a few months.

If that was the case, she didn't know what she was going to do. She needed to be de-virginized so Bonifay couldn't force her to marry Alphonse Picquet.

She needed to know what Buck's problem was, but had no idea how to bring such a delicate subject up.

"Josie?" he said from just a few feet behind her.

Relief swept through her. He was going to explain.

She turned.

He leaned on the corral fence.

Aggie lumbered over for some petting, and Buck absent-mindedly stroked the gelding's neck.

"Yes?" she prompted.

He stared at her for a long moment, then his eyes shifted to the lake. "I don't..."

"Yes?" she asked when it became obvious he wasn't going to finish.

His gaze drifted down, then back to the lake, then to her, then quickly back to the lake. "I have some work to do in the trailer. Don't disturb me until I tell you it's okay."

Her jaw dropped. This was an explanation? "What about—"

He shoved away from the corral fence. "It'll just be another hour. You can fix lunch when I'm done."

"But—"

"I mean it. Don't disturb me."

Josie watched with narrowed eyes as he disappeared into the trailer. The lock slipped into place with a resounding click.

She'd married a man who was every bit as stubborn, arrogant and boorish as Prime Minister Bonifay.

What was she supposed to do now?

Bored the next morning—and worried—Josie wandered over to the corral and leaned against the fence. Aggie wasted no time clomping over to be petted.

She stroked a hand down his forehead to his muzzle. "You like having me around, don't you, boy? If only to feed and pet you. At least you want me to touch you. All my husband wants is a slave."

She glanced over her shoulder at the camper, which was closed up tight like yesterday. Like the man inside.

Buck had completely ignored their burst of passion, acting as if it had never happened. He came out of the trailer around one, then put her to work the rest of the afternoon.

Josie, on the other hand, couldn't get what had happened in the trailer yesterday out of her mind.

No experience in her life could compare. She wanted to repeat it, to finish it, to see if the rest of sex was as good as the beginning.

She sighed and crossed her arms over the fence, then laid her head on them.

Not much chance of that. Not with Mr. I-Can-Ignore-Anything as a husband. She'd married a human ostrich. That's why he hadn't recognized her. He probably always stayed in remote places like this, burying his head in the proverbial sand. He had no television and she hadn't seen a newspaper since the one he brought back the first day.

What was she going to do? Should she leave and find another husband?

Too late for that. First she'd have to annul this marriage, which would not only take time, but would drag her name into the courts. She was sure to be caught.

Besides, the thought of being as close to another man as she'd been to Buck made her want to take a cleansing swim in the cold waters of Lake Tahoe.

No, she had to stay married to Buck. At least she was hidden from Bonifay. And who knew? Perhaps she could break down Buck's resistance—sooner or later.

Aggie nudged her shoulder.

Josie lifted her arms and hugged him around his thick neck. "Aggie, Aggie, Aggie. You know what? I miss Montclaire. Especially Papa, even though he never talks to me. And Bayard and Alette. You don't know them, but I think you'd like them. Bayard is my brood stallion, and Alette is my favorite mare. I know I shouldn't brag, but a colt of theirs was ranked fifteenth in the U.S. Dressage Federation's Second Level last year."

Aggie nickered softly.

Josie smiled against his coat. "You say you'd like to meet them? That would be nice, but I don't think it's likely. Montclaire is a continent and two oceans away. I'll be going away in a few weeks, and we'll probably never see each other again."

She choked on the last words and again her gaze drifted

to the camper. Tears blurred the faded red outline as she realized she'd probably never see Buck again either, after she left.

Especially since they hadn't consummated the marriage. *Zut!*

She shoved away from the fence.

She had to stop dwelling on sex. She had to *do* something. Now.

Aggie whinnied his disappointment that she'd stopped petting him.

She focused her eyes on the gelding. "You fat old thing. You're bored, too, aren't you? Well, then, why don't you and I go for a ride?"

The thought of being on horseback again made Josie smile. Finally having a purpose, she turned toward the camper, then hesitated. Should she ask Buck's permission?

Her eyes narrowed. He didn't seem to care when he left her outside for hours, either working like a drudge or bored to tears. Besides, he'd told her expressly not to disturb him. So she wouldn't.

Her smile returning, Josie stepped around the camper and hauled down the ramp. She had to move the bag of oats and the grooming supplies to get to the saddle hanging on a rack at the front. The Western saddle was heavier than the English one she rode at home, but she'd saddled enough horses at Melissa's to be accustomed to the weight.

The camper door flew open as she passed on the way back to the corral, startling her into nearly dropping the saddle.

"What are you doing?" Buck demanded.

After giving him a glare for scaring her, Josie shifted the weight in her arms for a better grip. "I'm taking Aggie for a ride."

"The hell you are."

"The hell I'm not." She continued toward the corral.

"Aggie's an expensive rodeo mount. Not a pleasure riding horse."

She hefted the saddle up to rest on the top of the fence, then turned back to get the blanket and bridle. "Don't you know anything about horses? If all you do is ride him in the arena, he's going to go nuts on you. Every horse needs to get out on the trail every now and then and eat the roses."

"You mean smell the roses, don't you?"

She threw a wave at him. "Horses would rather eat roses than smell them. At least until they get to the first thorn."

She stepped into the back of the trailer, grabbed the tack, then climbed out and closed the ramp.

Having stepped out of the camper, Buck stood in her path, hands on his hips. "If you're going, I'm going with you."

She halted in front of him. "On one horse?"

"Aggie's big enough to carry both of us. We're not going far, and we're not going fast."

"Fine, but I call the saddle. You can sit on his ru…" Her voice trailed away as her gaze wandered to the open camper door and fell on an odd sight on the small table inside. "Is that a computer?"

Chapter Six

Buck bit back a curse and only resisted the overwhelming urge to reach over and yank the door shut because it would make him look guilty. The only thing he was guilty of was working.

Still, the shock on Josie's face and in her voice told him what he'd known for a long time—he was a deviant inside an anomaly.

Computer-literate cowboys were uncommon enough, usually limited to ranch owners or foremen who ran enough head to require a database to keep up with breeding and inoculation schedules. Rodeo cowboys who spent hours every day playing the stock market were rare enough to be considered freaks.

"What's it for?" she asked.

He considered lying, but quickly changed his mind. If he told her how he spent most of his days, she'd be even more shocked than she was now. Maybe this would finally drive her away. "I play the market."

He'd hidden the investor side of himself from the rodeo world so long, the words came out stiffly.

His rodeo buddies didn't know he had an M.B.A. from Wharton, didn't know he was worth several hundred million dollars, most of which he'd made on his own. They thought he was one of them—a poor cowboy wandering from rodeo to rodeo, living from paycheck to paycheck.

That's exactly what he wanted them to think, because in his mind, he was like them. He wore Wrangler jeans, drank beer, drove a Dodge truck and lived in a camper attached to his horse trailer. While he wasn't too crazy about the nomadic life of a rodeo cowboy, he'd loved the life of a real cowboy since working by his grandfather's side as a boy. He loved living where his closest neighbor was miles away, loved being out in the open air, even loved working with horses and cattle. They didn't care how much money you had, or how high up your name was on the social register.

But he also loved the excitement of playing the stock market. While other cowboys got their kicks from going head-to-head with a bull, he loved the thrill of pitting himself against a bull market.

Of course, he had the money to do it. Most cowboys didn't. Consequently, they didn't understand anything about it.

When he'd first returned to the Double Star after graduation, he'd tried discussing market trends with several ranch hands. They'd looked at him as if he were speaking Martian. He'd quickly learned that herding cows and market analysis didn't mix.

It was as if he lived in two completely different worlds. Yet he belonged to neither, because neither accepted both sides of him. His parents' world thought cowboys were in a class beneath them, and cowboys believed investors were an entirely different species.

"The stock market?" she asked, surprise clear in her voice.

"Is there another one?"

"Really?" Josie changed directions, stepping into the camper. She absently dropped the tack onto the couch that doubled as her bed and sat down in front of the computer. She studied the screen, then glanced up at him. "Do you really?"

Her disbelief offended him. "Why are you so surprised? Think I don't have enough brains to understand the difference between the Dow-Jones and the NASDAQ?"

She had the grace to look embarrassed as she returned her gaze to the screen. "Of course not. It's just that..."

"What?" he demanded when she trailed off.

"How do I put this delicately?" She cleared her throat. "It's just that I always thought you had to have lots of money to trade stocks."

If only she knew how much money he had. Suddenly he wanted her to know. He wanted to tell her exactly who he was, how much he was worth, how he'd doubled the fortune his grandfather had left him so many times he'd lost count. He wanted to impress her, to see her eyes light up at the mention of so much money.

In short, he wanted to show her he had the qualities she needed in a husband.

Could he be any stupider? He didn't want to be her husband for the rest of his life.

No, but he wanted *her*. Damn her luscious little princess hide.

Angry at her for making him want something he couldn't have, he pushed his hat back on his head. "Well, shucks, Mrs. Buchanan. You knowed when you married me that I ain't got two dimes to rub together."

She lifted her pert nose in the air and sniffed. "You don't have to go native on me. I'm sorry if I insulted you."

Buck backed off, realizing he was getting into deep water. He'd better start treading, or he was going to sink fast. For the first time since he'd met her, he didn't swim around the truth—he outright lied. "I don't have any money. This is sort of a practice site where you invest with play money."

Her eyes lit up. "Like Monopoly?"

Buck groaned inwardly. He should have known better than to think she'd be scared off by his investing. After all, she didn't know what constituted regular behavior for a cowboy.

He knew she'd been getting bored. Since he hadn't been able to scare her away, he'd decided to bore her until she left just to stay awake. Trouble was, she'd been keenly interested in every task he'd given her, no matter how hard or dirty. The only reason he could come up with why such an intelligent woman would find washing dishes and clothes fun was because those chores were new to her. She was starved for new experiences and for a princess, even the most mundane task was new.

For an excuse to turn away from her, he took off the hat he'd grabbed when he thought they were going for a ride and hung it on the hook by the door. "Yeah. Kinda like Monopoly."

"Can I play?"

Buck shook his head in disgust. He only had himself to blame.

"I can't?" she asked. "Why not?"

He turned back and studied her indignant face. If he was honest, he'd tell her she couldn't play with his stocks because it would keep her beside him, which he'd been avoiding as much as possible. That's why he'd spent so much time inside the trailer the last couple of days.

Usually, he checked his stocks only three or four times a day. The stock market wasn't how he'd made his fortune. Most of his money had come from investing in small companies that had a good product but no capital to mass-produce and market it.

The past two days, however, he'd been buying and selling ten times more than usual, just to keep himself from going crazy. Though the investing frenzy filled the time normally occupied by the tasks he'd given Josie, it wasn't doing much for his cell-phone bill.

But at the moment, his phone bill was the least of his worries. He could see the gears working in Josie's mind, figuring out a way to convince him to let her play with this new toy.

"There's no way I'm going to talk you out of this, is there?" he asked.

She grinned, obviously pleased with herself for being so obstinate.

He rolled his eyes, mostly at himself for also being proud of her tenacity. "Scoot over, then."

She made room for him on the table's bench seat.

He sat down and positioned the portable computer so she could see the screen, but he could still use the keyboard and touchpad.

"How much do you know about on-line investing?" he asked.

She twisted her mouth into a wry grimace. "Next to nothing."

Good. Then she wouldn't be able to figure out that the site was his personal account, set up through his own brokerage firm.

He cleared his throat in preparation for a lot of lying. "This is a site where people go who don't have any money but want to see how they'd do if they did, or for people who want to practice before they invest—to see if they're any good before they risk real money."

There really was such a site, set up by a broker in his firm to teach her teenage son's finance class the ins and outs of investing.

"How much do they give you to play with?"

"Well. How about we give you ten thousand to start off?" He was giving her his own money to "play" with, but what the hell. It was just money. Maybe if she was occupied trading stocks, she wouldn't be tempting him to do things he shouldn't—like taking her on the kitchen counter.

"The amount doesn't matter since it isn't real, does it?"

"Right. Okay. First a strategy lesson. Simply put, the object of the game is to buy low and sell high. Sounds easy, doesn't it?"

"No." She wrinkled her nose. "How do you know whether a stock is going to go up or down?"

He grinned. "You don't. That's the fun."

"Fun? Losing money is fun?"

"No, but making money is."

"What happens if you lose all your practice money?"

He shrugged. "I guess I—" He cleared his throat again. "Well. You have to quit for the day, but tomorrow you can have some more."

She smiled. "This *is* like Monopoly."

He shook his head. "In Monopoly, you'd buy, say, Boardwalk outright and own it. In the market, you buy just a little piece of a company. Also, the price of Boardwalk stays the same, no matter how many times you play. In the stock market, prices never stay the same. Look here." He pointed to a field on the screen where the number changed every two or three seconds. "This is an oil stock I've been watching."

"Do you have money invested in it?"

"Not yet. It's been dropping all day."

"It's losing money, and you want to invest in it?"

"Most of the time when a stock falls, it's going to rise again. You're just gambling on how low it's going to go. Though in this particular case, there's a reason this oil stock is losing money and a reason it's going to rise."

"There is? What?"

"Their first-quarter earnings statement came out yester-day, and the company lost money. Therefore, it's losing investors. But I know something most other investors don't. Not yet."

"What?"

"The company nailed a new market for their product this morning. The stock won't go down much longer before it starts going back up. I'm waiting for another fifty-cent drop, then I'm going to buy. If it doesn't start rising before then, that is."

"How did you know that?"

"What? About their new market?"

"Yes."

"I... Well. I keep up with the news."

Buck cussed inwardly. He hoped his succinct explanation satisfied her because he couldn't tell her he belonged to a very exclusive, very expensive news service that gleaned financial information from around the globe and got it to their customers before it came out in the regular media. Most of the news was trivial, but the service had paid for itself many times over by providing tidbits like this oil com-pany finding a new market.

Josie nodded thoughtfully, evidently accepting his an-swer. "What do I do?"

"Since we only have one computer, only one of us can play at a time, so why don't you watch me for a while? After I buy this oil stock, I'll help you set up your account."

An hour later, Buck bought thirty thousand shares of the oil stock.

"How can you afford so much if you only get ten thou-sand dollars to play with?" she asked.

He almost kissed her in appreciation of her quick mind. But he also had to think quick to cover his gaffe. "I've been playing for months. Your earnings accumulate."

"You've won that much money in the stock market?"

"You don't win it, you earn it. And yes, I've earned that much and more. I have investments in other stocks as well."

She grinned. "Don't you wish the money was real?"

If she only knew.

When his transaction went through, Buck started an account for Josie by transferring some of his reserve into a new account. He used his own social-security number, since he knew she didn't have one. She wasn't an American citizen, after all.

Or maybe she was. He didn't know if citizenship was automatic when a foreigner married an American, or if they still had to apply for citizenship.

When he'd set up the account, he slid the computer in front of her. He got her started by showing her a couple of stocks he'd had his eye on that day.

She watched them fall for half an hour. Then she bought a hundred shares of each. One of them started rising ten minutes later. The other fell a bit more, then started rising, too.

Josie was fascinated by the process, and Buck was fascinated by her. He watched her more than the screen. Whether she lost his money or made more was irrelevant. What mattered was she was having a good time. And she was.

He loved her tiny gasps of delight when her chosen stocks rose, the unconscious way she grabbed his sleeve when one took a small dip, the soft brush of her breast against his arm when she turned to him for a question.

By the time his stomach started growling, she'd made a little under a thousand dollars.

Josie blinked up at him. "You're hungry."

He knew how it was when you stared at a computer screen too long. Hard to adjust the eyes to reality. "I guess I am."

Her eyes shifted to the clock behind him. "It's almost one o'clock. I'd better start lunch."

He shrugged. "The market's gonna close at one, anyway."

"So early? Why?"

"It's in New York City. It's almost four there."

"Oh. That's right. We have Pacific time." Her narrowed gaze returned to his. "This is why you've been locked in here every day until one o'clock."

He shrugged. It was mostly to get away from her—or rather, the temptation of her. But he couldn't tell her the stock market was merely the means to that end.

"Why didn't you tell me about this earlier? I've been bored stiff most of the time. When I wasn't being worked to death, that is."

He ignored her sarcasm. "I didn't know you'd like it so much."

And he didn't know it would turn him on so much, to watch her clever mind quickly catch the nuances of the game and work through the options she had in each situation.

"I think I like it as much as you do."

"It's the most fun you can have with your clothes on." Too late, he realized that with this woman, the line he'd been using since college had a whole new meaning. Better distract her. "I also thought you might consider it strange."

"What's strange?"

"A cowboy playing the stock market."

She blinked. "Is it?"

"There aren't many cowboys out there with enough money."

"You don't have the money, either."

He looked away from her clear gaze. "No."

"But that doesn't stop you."

He was uncomfortable with the lies, and his stomach

growled right on cue. "Didn't someone mention something about lunch?"

She grinned. "Can we play again tomorrow?"

He restrained a groan with an effort. "I reckon."

"What time does the market open?"

"Too early. What's for lunch?"

She crinkled her nose at him. "Beef. What else? It's the only thing you buy for me to cook."

"Steak?" he asked hopefully.

"Steak tonight. Now we're having hamburgers."

He nodded and stood to let her rise from the bench.

He backed out of the stock-market software as she started rattling pots and pans. Then he shut down the computer. He quickly slid the cell phone he'd kept hidden behind the computer into his pocket so she wouldn't start asking questions about how he could afford one.

She was too smart, this princess of his.

Unfortunately, he loved every minute of it.

Josie craned her neck from her anonymous perch in the front seat of Buck's pickup, trying to catch all of the activity around her.

Friday night at the local drive-in movie. Could anything be more ordinary than this?

When Buck had asked her if she wanted to come, she'd jumped at the chance to experience a part of Americana she'd only seen in films—especially since he'd told her that this was their last night at the campground in Tahoe. The next day they were heading to a rodeo in Sonora, California, where he was scheduled to wrestle another steer.

Josie was a little anxious about entering the real world again, but he'd scoffed at the idea of her father being able to find her in a crowd at such a small, relatively obscure rodeo.

Of course, he didn't know it wasn't her father looking for

her. It was Bonifay. Not only would Montclaire's prime minister have had her picture all over the media every day he could manage it, by now he would have enlisted the aid of the American FBI.

But she didn't have to worry about being caught tonight. No one was going to recognize her as long as she stayed safely inside the truck. She could relax and enjoy herself at least one more night, and she was determined to do just that.

As she looked around, a station wagon pulled into a slot in front of her. Five children spilled out, ranging in age from about three to around twelve. They chased each other around the car, probably excited about watching the movie. The mother and father kept an eye on them as they filled the next space with seven lawn chairs, then dragged out a cooler and lumpy plastic bag, obviously filled with home-made popcorn.

In a beat-up old car three slots to Josie's right, a young couple was already going at each other hot and heavy. Two young girls stood outside the car, giggling at the lovers.

Down the row to the left, a truck had backed into the space. An overweight, middle-aged couple lounged in its bed, ensconced in lawn chaises and dining on submarine sandwiches and beer.

The smells of hot dogs, buttered popcorn and exhaust fumes drifted in through the open windows. Josie closed her eyes and breathed deeply. This was real life.

"Hey! Wake up and open the door!"

She opened her eyes to see Buck at the driver's side door, his arms laden with goodies from the concession stand. She quickly leaned over and shoved the door open.

He laid his booty on the seat—a huge container of pop-corn, plus two soft drinks, hot dogs and candy bars.

"*Mon Di—*" She cut off the automatic French. "My God, Buck. We finished dinner just two hours ago."

He grinned. "I know. But this is movie food. It doesn't count."

Josie slid the cardboard tray into the middle of the seat. She popped a kernel of popcorn into her mouth. Light and fluffy, it had just the right amount of salt and butter.

"I can just imagine how fattening this is," she muttered as Buck settled behind the wheel.

"Like I said, it's movie food. It—"

"Doesn't count. I heard you. I only hope my thighs did."

"Your thighs look pretty good to me." He grabbed a handful of popcorn. "Besides, you've worked hard enough today to earn a few calories."

She peered closely at him. It was the first compliment he'd given her, but he wasn't even looking at her thighs. He seemed to toss the compliment at her with as much thought as he'd toss a kernel of popcorn to a pigeon. Though the fact that he'd complimented her thighs at all proved he'd been thinking about them.

Why couldn't he be straightforward about his desire?

And why couldn't he do something about it?

She couldn't keep the edge from her voice as she said, "That's true enough, thanks to you."

"Hey, would you rather sit on your butt all day and eat bonbons?"

She sniffed. "No. Bonbons are even more fattening."

He smiled around a mouthful of popcorn. "I don't know what you're complaining about. I brought you to the movies tonight, didn't I? Hell, sweetheart. You made almost two thousand dollars in the stock market this morning. You deserve a night out."

His reminder of the excitement she'd felt when the market closed mollified her, though she twisted her mouth wryly. "It wasn't two thousand *real* dollars."

"Maybe not." He glanced down as he snagged another handful of popcorn. "But you did good, all the same."

"I *am* rather proud of myself. If only I could..." She stopped herself before she could finish the sentence. *If only I could invest Montclaire's money so successfully.*

"If only you could what?"

She took another handful of popcorn. "Nothing."

"Well, you should be proud. You caught on a helluva lot quicker than I did when I first started."

"When did you start?"

He'd shoved popcorn into his mouth, so she had to wait until he'd finished chewing. "Several years ago."

"Why?"

"Why what?"

"If it's so unusual for a cowboy to play the stock market, how did you get started?"

"Aren't you full of questions."

She shrugged. "I'm curious. And perhaps you don't remember, but I *am* your wife. I should know about you."

He'd reached for his soft drink, but instead of bringing it to his mouth, he set it on his thigh and stared for a long moment out the windshield. Finally, he gave her a piercing look. "You'll be gone in a few months. What does it matter?"

Suddenly all of the questions she'd been asking herself the past few days were answered. She knew why he'd been keeping her at a distance all week, why he was working them both to exhaustion, why they hadn't made love.

He was worried about the same thing she was—falling in love with someone who wouldn't be around long.

At least, that was the most logical explanation.

The possibility endeared him to her and seemed to forge a bond between them.

"I'd like to know." Her words were absolutely sincere. She didn't know enough about his life to satisfy her insatiable curiosity.

They usually talked every evening after dinner, sitting in

the lawn chairs and watching the stars pop out. But Buck had talked in circles about his past. The problem was, she'd been too busy with circles of her own to notice—until now. She wondered what he was hiding. Surely his deep, dark secret couldn't be as big as hers.

"Do you really, Josie?" he asked quietly, still holding her gaze. "Do you want to know *everything* about me?"

His voice was low and sexy. The sound, and the way he looked at her, made her own voice breathless as she answered, "Yes, Buck. Everything."

"I—"

Suddenly the speaker hanging on Josie's lowered window blared to life, startling her. The hand she'd lowered into the popcorn jumped, scattering kernels all over the seat.

"Zu— Oh, no." She scooped up popcorn until Buck's hand on her wrist stopped her. Her gaze rose to his. "What?"

Buck studied Josie's bright, beautiful face in the light of the concession commercial playing on the screen. The dancing soft drink and popcorn box were the only things that had saved him from telling her everything.

Every day, he hated lying to her more. Every day, he wanted her more. Not just her body—though he desperately wanted to feel her long, luscious curves beneath him.

He wanted all of Josie.

She'd been such a good sport while they'd been camped by Lake Tahoe. She worked hard, took his abuse good-naturedly and, best of all, she loved playing the stock market.

He'd never met another woman like her, and he was afraid he never would again.

"Buck, the butter might ruin the leather."

He shook off the disturbing thoughts and released her. He turned his attention to the screen while she cleaned up the mess.

Halfway through the first preview, she turned down the volume on the speaker. "Well?"

"Well, what?" he asked gruffly without taking his eyes from the screen.

"I thought we were going to talk."

"The movie's starting."

"But this is just a—"

"Turn the sound back up, will you?"

She hesitated for a long moment, during which he could feel her eyes on him. Then she returned the volume to an audible level and settled back on the seat.

Buck kept his eyes forward as the previews gave way to the feature presentation—an action-adventure film his rodeo buddies had raved about. But his attention wasn't on the movie. He couldn't concentrate on anything with Josie sitting so close.

Though his eyes were turned toward the screen, he watched her out of the corner of his eye. He knew every time she lifted popcorn to her mouth, every time she licked salt off her fingers. Despite the bullets and explosions rattling the speaker against the window, he was aware of her every breath, every crunch of her teeth on the popcorn.

He kept eating, to keep his hands from reaching for her, but he didn't taste anything.

He tried to remember all the reasons he had for not sleeping with her, but reason seemed distant and obscure when she was so close and so real.

Once their hands touched when they both reached for popcorn at the same time. With a tiny gasp, she quickly drew her hand away. He ached to grab it and press a kiss on her palm, then lick every grain of salt from her fingers, then from her lips, then—

He cussed under his breath and shifted in his seat.

Damn, it was getting hot in here.

He rolled his window all the way down and took a long

swig of his soft drink. He decided to let her have the rest of the popcorn, and reached for a hot dog instead. He polished it off as a building exploded on the screen, then ate the other one. Half an hour later, when she'd made no move toward them, he downed both candy bars.

"I'm going to toss all this in that trash can over there," she said during a lull in the intense action. "If you're finished."

He sucked the last ounce of soft drink from his cup, then added it to the stack. He watched her instead of the screen. She carefully kept her head down as she ran to the trash can and back.

"Thanks," he said as she climbed back into her seat.

"It's woman's work, isn't it?" she asked with a hint of sarcasm.

He shrugged and returned his attention to the screen. A second later, he felt her hand groping along his lap.

Chapter Seven

Startled by Josie's touch, Buck flinched. "What the—"

She held up the kernel of popcorn she'd plucked from a crease in his jeans.

"Oh." He released the breath he'd sucked in. So it wasn't a blatant attempt at seduction. She was just tidying up some more. Damn. "Thanks."

Instead of tossing it out the window for the birds, she scooted closer and held it to his lips. "Here."

Her voice, a notch lower than usual, hit him like a hard fist in his gut. He met her gaze in the flashing lights from the screen.

Her expression was uncertain, but there was a degree of determination that made his lips curve.

Maybe she *was* trying to seduce him. He hoped so.

He was tired of their relationship the way it was. He was sick of making her work like a dog, sick of having to keep his hands off her. He wanted more. Much, much more.

And if he succumbed to the seduction of a beautiful woman, who could blame him? He was a saint to have lasted this long.

Her hand began to falter.

He grabbed her wrist and brought the popcorn to his lips. Holding her gaze, he opened his mouth and inserted her fingers inside. His teeth gently scraped along the fingers that held the kernel, then his tongue delved between them to flick the treat into his mouth.

She gasped softly.

He pulled her fingers out and chewed the kernel slowly, holding her wrist captive. After he'd swallowed the popcorn, he drew her fingers back into his mouth—one by one—to suck, lick and nibble them until no taste of butter or salt remained.

"Buck..." she whispered. "Please."

"Such manners," he said as he concentrated on her pinkie. "You know what I think?"

"What?"

"I think you're trying to seduce me."

She didn't try to deny it. "Can I?"

He chuckled. "Are you asking permission, or whether it's possible?"

"Both."

He drew her hand down to the growing evidence of his desire. "What do you think?"

He almost came unglued when instead of shying away, her warm fingers lingered to follow the ridge in his jeans.

"Mon Dieu. C'est beau."

He choked on a smile. For once she didn't notice she'd slipped into French.

Unable to endure her caresses without exploding, he grabbed her exploring hand and brought it to his lips to place a kiss on the inside of her wrist. Then he drew her arm around his neck, placed his hands on her waist and dragged her across the seat until her hip bumped against his.

He covered her gasp with his mouth. No peck this time. He kissed her the way he had the day before, the way he'd been dying to do since he'd sworn off her the moment he found out who she was.

Who she was didn't matter at the moment. He could barely remember who *he* was. Especially when her response was so unrestrained, so intoxicating, so passionate.

She locked her arms around his neck and pulled his mouth down to hers. When he slid his tongue along her lips, seeking entrance to the warm, wet recesses of her mouth, she opened them willingly, moaning when he wrapped his tongue around hers.

He moaned, too, and pressed her closer, but their positions didn't give him the pressure he craved.

So he scooped her onto his lap while he slid from under the steering wheel.

As he leaned her back against his arm, she shifted, looping her arm around his neck, causing her bottom to scrape against him.

He clamped his other arm across her legs, holding her still, and dragged in a deep, hissing breath.

She froze. "Did I do something wrong?"

"No, sweetheart." He pushed a strand of black hair off her face. "I've just waited so damn long. I'm ready to explode."

"Me, too." She rubbed a hand along his jaw. "Can we explode together?"

"If we do it right and, sweetheart, I'm planning on it."

He kissed her again, long and hard, then trailed kisses down her neck. Frustrated when he ran out of skin at the top button of her shirt, he raised his hand to unfasten it, but he got sidetracked when his fingers brushed against the mound of her breast.

She moaned when he molded his hand to the gently heaving curves, then cried his name when he brushed his thumb across the tip. He didn't know what fascinated him more—the passionate sounds she was making, or the way her hands roamed over his neck and chest, or the nub that was forming under his thumb.

The sound of her, the smell of her, the taste of her, the feel of her, the sight of her—all his senses combined to heat his blood, boiling rational thought until it was nothing but steam, which floated right out the window.

Before he knew it, he had her lying half beneath him on the seat, her blouse unbuttoned. He was working on getting her bra unhooked—vowing to buy out the nearest Victoria's Secret's stock of front-closure bras in her size—when his knee hit the horn on the steering wheel.

The sound blasted across the movie lot.

He ducked, knowing every eye around would be on his truck. "Damn."

Beneath him, Josie said in a muffled, amused voice, "Well, that was subtle."

He leaned his forehead against hers and chuckled. "I thought the movie sound effects needed some excitement."

A particularly loud explosion blared through the speaker, and she laughed. "They are a little dull, aren't they?"

He lifted his head to peer down at her. Disheveled and half-naked, she was the most beautiful sight he'd ever seen. "You care anything about this movie?"

She scraped her nails through his hair. "What movie?"

"Let's go home before they start selling tickets to watch us."

"All right."

He all but leaped into the driver's seat to start the engine.

Josie began buttoning her blouse. "Oh, Buck? Shouldn't we hang the speaker up?"

"Hell. I forgot about the speaker." He reached for the latch on his door, but she stopped him with a hand on his shoulder.

"I'll do it."

She opened the door carefully and squeezed through an

impossibly small crack. She lifted the speaker off the window, hung it on its hook, then climbed back in. As soon her door closed, he shoved the pickup into gear and stepped on the gas. He drove as fast as he could and still not run over people.

As soon as he cleared the exit, he grabbed her thigh. "Why are you sitting so far away?"

"It's where I've been—" she gasped as he dragged her across the seat, smack against his side "—sitting all week."

"It's too damn far."

She sighed happily and leaned against him. "You're right."

He leaned down to give her a brief, hard kiss. "God, you taste good."

"Like buttered popcorn?"

He chuckled low and kissed her again. "Yeah."

"Fancy that."

She rubbed his thigh as he drove twenty miles over the speed limit toward Lake Tahoe. He wrapped his arm around her when he didn't have to change gears.

"Buck?" she said after a long, silent moment.

"Yes, sweetheart?"

She rubbed her cheek on his shoulder. "Thank you for coming to your senses before we...well, you know. I don't want my first time to be all cramped inside a truck." She laughed softly and pushed her hand inside his shirt, which she'd halfway unbuttoned at some point. "You're so big, your feet would've had to stick out the window. I think the people in the cars around us would've guessed what we were doing, don't you?"

Buck didn't hear her last few sentences. His mind caught on the words *first time*.

He cleared his throat. "You mean that this is your first time with me, right? Not that it's your first time."

"No. This is my first time. I've never had sex."

"Ever?"

"Isn't that what *never* means?"

A blast of icy water cooled his raging libido.

She was a virgin. Why hadn't that occurred to him before?

Because she didn't act like a virgin, that's why. She was too damn good at making him want her. Then there was the fact that she was just a few weeks shy of twenty-five. How many twenty-five-year-old virgins existed nowadays?

But she was a princess. Her virginity was probably a state treasure. She would have been protected from seduction all her life.

She must have felt the sudden tension in him, because she lifted her head and asked, "Are you all right?"

No! he wanted to shout. *Why are you doing this to me? Did you walk into my life just so you could tear me apart?*

If he was fair, he'd acknowledge the fact that she didn't know how much he wanted her—and how much he *didn't* want her.

But he sure as hell wasn't feeling fair. Not when he ached to bury himself deep inside her and stay there for the next millennium.

Damn her for being the only woman he'd ever wanted to keep, and for being the one woman he couldn't have. Damn himself for marrying a woman he knew nothing about. Damn her father for allowing her to run away. Damn her country for having a stupid law about the heir marrying before age twenty-five, which made her run away in the first place. Damn his parents for making him hate the life she leads.

He knew he shouldn't let his parents' life-style keep him from having the woman he loved. That meant he was letting them win. But—

His thoughts came to a screeching halt. Had the word *love* just popped into his head?

"Buck?" Josie leaned forward and peered at him closely. "What's wrong?"

Panic raced through him like wildfire. It made his voice gruff. "Nothing."

"You haven't changed your mind, have you?"

There was no way in hell he was making love to her now. Consummating the marriage was risky enough. Consummating it with a virgin princess would ensure he'd be stuck with her forever. If there weren't laws about this kind of thing in the United States, there probably were in her country.

But beyond that was his own moral code. He might be able to endure the censure of his parents, maybe even the disapproval of the world, but he wouldn't be able to live with himself if he took her virginity, then left her. Especially when he knew that if Picquet was an acceptable husband, he would be, too.

"Josie, let's talk about—"

"No!" she cried. "Please, Buck. You have to make love to me."

"I'm sorry, but—"

"You wanted to five minutes ago." She twisted on the seat to face him. "What happened?"

"That's before I knew you were a virgin."

She threw her hand in the air. "What the hell does that have to do with anything?"

He considered telling her the truth, telling her he knew who she was. But he was afraid that would send her scurrying away, and the thought of her leaving made him want to drive his truck head-on into the next tree.

"You said yourself, this marriage isn't permanent."

"No, it isn't." Her voice sounded sad, which touched his heart. "But I need you to make love to me. Don't you see? If my...father finds me before we consummate this marriage, he'll have it annulled and make me marry...the man he's picked out for me.''

"Your father must be very rich.''

She went still. "What makes you say that?''

"Nowadays—in this country, at least—arranged marriages only occur when there's a lot of money involved.'' He added bitterly, "Or social status. But that usually involves money, too.''

She studied him so curiously, he pressed, "Well, is he?''

She dropped her gaze. "I guess some people would think he's rich. But his...company is about to go bankrupt. He needs money to make it solvent. The man I'm supposed to marry has promised to invest a lot of money in the company.''

"But you don't like this guy.''

"No, but that's not why I refuse to marry him.'' She met his eyes squarely. "I have evidence that he's planning to ruin Mont—um, my father's company.''

Buck didn't doubt it. Picquet never did anything unless it was going to bring him personal—which meant monetary—gain. "And that's why you need a rich husband. So he can invest his money and you won't have to marry this guy.''

"Yes.''

So she wasn't refusing to marry Picquet just because he was old, ugly and had nasty sexual habits. She was trying to save her country. At least, she thought she was trying to save her country. He hadn't heard anything about Picquet's plans for Montclaire. He'd have to check his sources.

But for the moment, Josie's altruism made his estimation of her rise still another notch, which didn't help matters. Though it explained why she'd been willing to put up with so much crap from him the past few days, it made him want her even more.

And it made it even more imperative that he not have

her—not unless he was willing to give up his own way of life to help her and her country.

And he wasn't.

God, that made him feel selfish. But he'd fought so long for the right to be what he wanted to be—a simple cowboy. He wasn't ready to give up his own dream for Josie's.

Why should he? Sure, he'd heard of Montclaire, but before a week ago, he'd never given a second thought to the tiny island country.

Besides, he could just imagine the ecstasies his mother would go into if she learned he was married to Princess Joséphene of Montclaire. Alicia Buchanan's social standing would soar beyond her wildest dreams. She'd actually be proud of her son for once.

Buck frowned. When held up next to Josie's selflessness, his motives seemed childish. Was he actually basing his happiness on whatever would give his parents the most grief?

He shifted in his seat. He had enough problems at the moment without psychoanalyzing himself. Right now he had to convince Josie that sex was the last thing she wanted.

Damn. Did he really have to do this?

"Sorry, sweetheart, but I'm not the husband you need."

"I know." Josie sighed heavily, as if carrying the weight of the world on her shoulders. Or the weight of a country. "I just need the time staying married to you will give me."

"I see."

"I also need you to make love to me."

"Josie…"

"Please, Buck. It's important. More important than you know."

He hated refusing her, and not just because of the desire gnawing at his gut. He wanted to please her, to make her happy.

Damn, he was further gone than he thought.

No! He wasn't. He couldn't be in love with Josie. She wasn't the kind of woman he wanted, not really. "Josie" was just a phase in Princess Joséphene of Montclaire's life—a brief respite before she went back to princessing.

So what if she seemed perfectly happy playing his little trailer-park queen? She was like a little girl playing house. She knew she had a royal palace to return to anytime she got tired of the game.

So what if she was the only woman he'd ever met who could make several thousand dollars in the stock market in the morning, then stockpile manure in the afternoon?

There *were* others like her out there. There had to be. He just hadn't looked hard enough.

"A man has principles, Josie," he told her finally. "If he doesn't live up to them, he's not worth very much as a man."

"Need I remind you that consummation was one of the conditions we agreed on when we married?"

"You can always get our marriage annulled and find some other dumb cowpoke who'll do the honors." He tried to make his shrug careless, to make her think her decision didn't matter to him one way or the other. He hoped she couldn't see the stiffness in the gesture.

He was more relieved than he should have been when she shook her head. "No, I can't. We'd have to go to court. He'd certainly find me then."

Her quick answer made him realize she'd already considered the possibility. He didn't like her thinking about leaving him.

"So what are you going to do?" he asked.

She sat back against the seat. "What options do I have?"

He didn't answer the rhetorical question.

A silent minute later, Josie asked quietly, "Don't you want to make love to me?"

God, she knew how to make him feel lower than grazed

grass. He reached over and gently squeezed her knee. "The answer to that is obvious. Or at least it was."

"Then there's hope," she murmured.

He straightened. "Pardon me?"

He'd heard her. He just wanted to know what she meant.

"Nothing."

His eyes narrowed. "Josie…"

"Are you sorry now that you left the movie?" she asked in a blatant attempt to change the subject.

"No. Now, tell me what—"

"You said your rodeo buddies recommended it highly."

"Damn it, Josie, I couldn't pay the slightest bit of attention to it with you wiggling all over the truck. Tell me—"

"Wiggling?" She smiled, obviously amused by his choice of words.

He was not amused. "Josie…"

She crossed her arms over her stomach. "What?"

"I meant what I said."

"I understand," she answered calmly.

He didn't believe either one of those words, but she obviously wasn't going to answer him. Damn. Now he had to worry about what kind of torture she was planning.

When they finally got to the campground, he told her go on in the camper while he checked on Aggie. The gelding was doing fine, of course, and after spending several minutes scratching behind his horse's ears, Buck wandered over to the side of the lake.

If Josie thought she could seduce him…

Hell. She probably could.

She had every reason to think she could. If they'd been at home tonight, nothing would have stopped him. He'd been that far gone.

He picked up a rock and flung it in the lake.

"Buck?" Josie called from the camper door. "Are you coming to bed?"

He didn't answer, and a minute later he heard her mutter something and close the door. He could imagine her getting ready for bed, taking off her clothes and sliding into the T-shirt he'd given her. She'd tuck the covers in tight, then slip between the sheets. She'd be soft and warm. And kissable. And—

"Hell."

He jerked off his boots and threw his hat on top of them. Then without removing another stitch, he walked into the freezing cold water of Lake Tahoe.

The next day, Buck squinted across the fairgrounds arena at Sonora, California. The trip south from Lake Tahoe had taken only a couple of hours, so they'd arrived in plenty of time for the Saturday afternoon event.

There weren't many people filling the stands yet. The majority were young women who talked in small groups, keeping indulgent eyes on children who chased each other around the stands. The rodeo didn't start for another half an hour, so the people in the stands were mostly ones who'd come with rodeo participants.

He hadn't really expected to see Josie. She'd told him she would join the crowd once the rodeo started, when it was dense enough to blend in.

Even though he knew he wouldn't be able to see her, Buck turned toward the lot behind the participants' entrance where his rig was parked. The one red corner he could see beckoned him—like the way a big package under a Christmas tree tempts a child. Everything he wanted was inside that aluminum box. All he had to do was open the door and take it.

Hell. He rubbed a hand down his face. The temptation was more like the sirens calling sailors to their doom.

"Hi, there, Buck."

Grateful for the distraction, Buck turned his attention

away from Josie. He smiled down at a diminutive blonde with whom he'd considered starting an affair. He'd met her several months before at the Tulare rodeo, and had seen her again at Prineville, Oregon. The green-eyed barrel racer was built just the way he liked his women, and seemed to have half a brain. Surely she could grasp the concepts of the stock market.

"Ramona. I was hoping you'd be here."

Ramona gave him a cat's smile. "You were?"

"You wanna go grab a soft drink before the party starts?"

"Well, I should be warming up my mare…" She reached for his hand. "But I'd rather spend the time with you, handsome."

As they meandered over to the concession stand, he asked about the rodeos she'd been to during the past few weeks, trying not to compare her height—Ramona's head topped off at his shoulder—with Josie's tall frame. He forced himself not to think about the crick he'd get in his neck if he tried to kiss her—or how easy it was to kiss Josie.

As they stood by the arena fence, watching the crowd file into the stands, Ramona gave him the perfect opening to bring up the subject on his mind by mentioning a large purse she'd won at the Red Bluff Roundup.

"Do you invest any of your winnings?" he asked with studied indifference.

"I'm saving as much as I can," she said. "For sort of a hope chest. When I find a fella to marry, I want us to have a place of our own."

"So you put your money in a savings account?"

She nodded and named a hometown bank.

"You get, what? About three percent interest?"

She shrugged. "I guess."

Not a good sign. She didn't even know how much interest she was paid on her savings account. "You know you'd get a much better return if you put your money in some safe stock.''

"Stock?" She frowned. "You mean cattle?"

He barely kept himself from groaning. He should probably drop the subject right there, but he couldn't. This was important. He had to prove Josie wasn't the only woman who liked both sides of him—the investor and the cowboy. "I'm talking about the stock market."

She didn't actually take a step away from him, but her mind sure did. "Stock market? You mean that Davy-Jones thing?"

He closed his eyes to keep them from rolling. "Dow-Jones."

"Oh, yeah, well, okay. Stock market, huh?" Her eyes darted everywhere but at him. "Say, you know? I really need to get back and warm up my mare."

He nodded. "Sure."

"I need to have a good ride and everything if I'm going to have a shot at the National Finals."

"I understand, Ramona."

"Maybe we can get together again sometime." She was already sidling away.

"Yeah, sure."

"'Bye."

She hurried away, and Buck leaned against the arena fence to finish his soft drink. He'd chased her off in record time.

Well, what did he expect? A miracle?

No. All he wanted was to find another woman like Josie.

Buck pushed away from the fence. He wasn't going to give up. Ramona wasn't the only woman around.

By the time hats came off for the Star Spangled Banner, Buck had tried the same approach with three other women— and even one man. He was met with blank stares, jokes or nervous smiles and decided to stop before the entire rodeo crowd decided he'd come from another planet.

He scanned the crowd filling the stands on the other side of the arena. He honed in on Josie in seconds, despite the disguise she'd attempted. Shoving her hair up into her hat and wearing no makeup, loose jeans and a faded chambray shirt might fool people who weren't looking for her, but he knew her form too well.

He shook his head in disgust. If he could recognize her this quickly in that crowd, he was already too far gone. He felt like a mother who could pick out her newborn in a hospital nursery housing fifty babies. There was some sort of intangible, but very real, connection tying them together.

Damn. He needed to get out of this marriage as soon as possible.

As soon as the thought flashed across his mind, every instinct inside him shouted, "No!"

Which scared the bejeezus out of him.

So what the hell was he supposed to do now? He either had to give her up or give in to the fate destiny was leading him to.

In other words, he was damned if he did and damned if he didn't.

"Hey, Buck!" Loy Osman slapped him on the back. "You rob Fort Knox or something?"

"Fort Knox?" Buck turned from tightening Aggie's cinch to face the bull rider he'd known for years. Loy was nearly a foot shorter than Buck and weighed about eighty pounds less, but he was a damn fine cowboy.

Loy nodded in the direction of the rodeo office. "A couple of guys came in there a minute ago, says they's looking for you. FBI, they says."

"FBI!" Damn. "Looking for me? What for? Did they say?"

Loy shrugged. "Mena asked 'em, but they wasn't saying much. Something about questions is all. What's up?"

"Hell if I know," Buck said. "But I'm not sticking around to find out, if you get my drift."

Because of a tendency to bust either jaws or speed limits, there was no love lost between most rodeo cowboys and the law. Loy had been caught on both counts. "What can I do to help?"

"You think the guys'll stall 'em?"

"You know rodeo cowboys, Buck. When it comes to cops, we can stonewall with the best."

"You're not up first in bull-riding, are you?"

Loy shook his head. "Dead last."

Buck craned his neck to peer into the arena. "Good. They haven't even finished with the bareback riding yet. You've got time."

"For what?"

"To deliver a message for me."

Josie didn't get worried until the cowboy who'd been scanning the crowd started excusing himself down her row. She gripped the rough plank stadium seat, but kept her eyes on the bronc rider picking himself up from the dirt of the arena and dusting himself off.

Was the cowboy coming for her? There was room on either side of her for someone to sit, but there were other rows with empty space, too. What should she do? Get up and move in the other direction? Or wait and see what he was up to?

Before she could make a decision, he sat next to her.

"Are you Miss Josie?"

She stared at him, unable to reply, uncertain whether or not she'd been caught. He'd used the name Josie, but that could mean anything.

"Don't worry," he said in a low voice. "I'm Loy Osman, a friend of Buck's."

He sprang to his feet as the next bronc rider shot from the gate. "That's the way! Ride that son of a gun, Kevin. You've got him! You've got him!" The buzzer sounded. "All right!"

He settled back onto the seat. "Sorry 'bout that. He's a friend of mine."

"Does Buck need something?"

Loy leaned close. "Ol' Buck needs to hightail it outta here. Seems the FBI's wanting to ask him a few questions."

Josie would have jumped from her seat, but Loy grabbed her arm and held her down. "Uh-uh, little lady. You're to go nice and quiet-like, so's you don't attract any attention. Understand?"

She nodded, her heart bucking like the bronc in the arena.

Loy patted her arm. "Look over to your left. You see that gate yonder? On the other side of that taco stand? Buck said for you to mosey on down thataway. He'll pick you up there. You've got plenty of time. Probably another ten minutes. He's got to load his horse first. That's what he's doing now."

Josie took a deep breath. "I understand. Slow and easy. Like I'm just going down to get a taco."

"You got it."

"Loy?"

"Yes, ma'am?"

"Thank you. I won't forget your help."

He grinned. "Well, that's enough reward right there, to know a bee-yoo-tiful lady's never gonna forget me."

"Goodbye, Loy."

"'Bye, Miss Josie."

She made her exit the next time the crowd stood to cheer a bronc rider. She walked down the seat in front of her, vacated by the standing people. By the time they began to sit back down, she'd reached the aisle.

She felt conspicuous as she made her way down the stairs and kept her head low, grateful for the wide-brimmed hat that shaded her face. People were constantly scanning the crowd, looking for friends or family or trying to remember where they were sitting, so it was hard to tell if any of them were FBI. If they were, they were dressed as cowboys. In this crowd, a suit and tie would stick out like a storm cloud on a blue horizon.

When she made the taco stand in a couple of minutes, she decided to use the ladies' room so she wouldn't have to wait around the gate. The line was a few people deep, so she made it out in time to see Buck's rig inching along the chain-link fence toward the gate.

She had to quell the instinct to run, knowing it would only draw attention. Forcing herself to take long, deep breaths, she sauntered toward the gate as if she had all the time in the world.

Fortunately, she wasn't the only one leaving. A young couple with a squalling baby pushed a stroller past the ticket-takers. Josie walked right behind, as if she was with them, then veered to the right.

Buck waited a few yards down the fence. Josie walked quickly toward his truck.

As she reached for the door, she heard the distinct whir and click of a camera. She'd heard the sound so often in her lifetime, there was no mistaking it.

But a lifetime of dealing with intrusive reporters also made her shy away from cameras, so instead of turning toward the noise, she yanked open the door and jumped in.

"Go!" she cried without thinking. "A photographer."

Buck stepped on the gas, but latecomers to the rodeo kept him from leaving quickly.

The photographer caught up easily. "Princess!" he called. "Princess Joséphene!"

Chapter Eight

Josie's heart sank as she showed the photographer the back of her hat instead of her face. Damn the media. There was no way she could pass this off as another case of mistaken identity.

Buck grabbed her shoulder and pushed her down on the seat. "Get down, princess. I'll get us out of here."

Princess. He knew! Josie felt like crying. The charade was over. Was the marriage over, too? So soon?

A few minutes of crazy driving later, Buck said, "All right. I think we've lost them."

Josie sat up slowly, adjusting the hat he'd knocked askew. They drove in silence several minutes. At last, in a small, miserable voice, she said, "I'm Princess Joséphene."

"Well, there's a news flash."

She peered at him sharply. "You know?"

"Yes, sweetheart. I know."

"How long have you known?"

"Since the morning after we got married."

She thought back. "When my picture was in the newspaper."

"It was damn hard to miss."

"You lied to me."

"And you haven't lied to me?" He gave her a hard look, then turned his attention back to the road. "Let's just say I went along with your little game, okay?"

She winced. "I wish it were just a game."

"I know why you're running," he said quietly. "But I didn't then. I thought you were just a spoiled little girl who was throwing a tantrum."

"That's why you worked me like a slave, isn't it? To make me run back to Montclaire."

"Yes."

"Well, I didn't."

"No, sweetheart, you didn't." He smiled, looking almost as if he were proud of her.

Well, she was proud of herself. She'd shown this cowboy that a princess can get her hands dirty just like anyone else. "So what now?"

His smile vanished. "What do you mean, 'what now?'"

The hat made her head feel as if it weighed a hundred pounds. She took it off and laid it on the seat between them. Her hair fell around her shoulders. She pushed it to one side so she could rub the back of her neck. "I don't want to cause any trouble for you, Buck."

"You let me take care of myself, all right?"

"That's what I want you to do. The FBI's involved now. You don't need to go to prison for my sake."

"Nobody's going to prison. What laws have we broken? I didn't kidnap you. Hell, if anything, you're the one who shanghaied me."

"You don't know Prime Minister Bonifay. I'm sure he can talk the American government into finding some law that would put you away. And you don't have the money to fight the lawyers he could hire."

He shrugged. "I've got a few dollars stashed away."

"No, Buck. I'm not going to let you spend your hard-earned money on me. Why don't you just let me off at the next town? I'll find some way to—"

"No!" he roared. "Damn it, Josie. I'm not about to let you g—" He cut himself off abruptly and shoved the shift into the next highest gear. "I'm not going to abandon a lady in need. My grandpa's ghost would haunt me 'til the day I die."

"But I—"

"Just shut up. You're staying right where you are and that's the end of the discussion."

Relieved, she sank against the seat with a sigh. She didn't want to cause him trouble, but she didn't want to be on her own, either. She only had a few dollars left and only a vague idea of where she was. Plus, she wouldn't know who to trust. She trusted Buck.

I'm not going to abandon a lady in need.

Not exactly a pledge of undying devotion. Still, his vehemence warmed her heart.

Then the word *lady* caught in her mind. She gave him a sour look. "Lady? Since when have you treated me like a lady?"

He relaxed visibly, apparently convinced she'd accepted that he wasn't going to desert her. "Oh, I can think of several times when I treated you exactly like a lady."

"You may have treated me like a woman, but not a lady."

"Lady, huh?" He glanced in the side mirror, then at her. "Is that what you want, Princess? For me to wait on you hand and foot?"

"No, I..." Josie's words drifted off. He knew she wanted to be treated like an ordinary woman? "I thought you made me work so hard because you wanted me to leave."

He shrugged. "I quickly realized that wasn't working. The harder I made you work, the more you liked it."

"I've never minded hard work. In fact, I'm much more comfortable grooming the horses than grooming myself for a state function."

His face seemed to harden and soften at the same time. After a quiet moment, he said, "Working with horses is the only thing you do, isn't it?"

"Since other royals have similar interests, it was deemed acceptable. Though very few of them work at it as hard as I do." She turned to stare out the windshield. "Besides my horses, all I do is dress up and play princess."

"Won't you be ruling your country one day?"

"That's the plan, supposedly."

"Shouldn't you be learning something about ruling?"

Her jaw muscles tightened, which lifted her chin. "Yes."

"But Bonifay won't let you."

She winced. "I keep blaming Bonifay, but the truth is, it's my fault. I should've forced my way into power when I realized how thoroughly Bonifay had usurped my father's place."

"But you don't like power."

She turned to him. "How do you know that?"

He shrugged. "I don't like power, either. It's hard enough to control my own life, much less other people's. It's why I live the way I do."

Josie sank back against the seat.

A princess and a cowboy. Worlds apart, yet they had so much in common. He understood her completely, after just a week together.

Was it possible he felt a connection to her, something more than this marriage bargain they'd made?

Was it possible he loved her as much as she loved him?

Mon Dieu. She'd said it.

Though she'd suspected the thought was rattling around in her brain for several days now, she'd never let it surface, believing that if she never uttered the words, never even thought them, they couldn't be true.

But they were. She loved this man. This poor, sweet rodeo cowboy.

Zut! How could she have let this happen? She'd known all along that she'd never be allowed to keep him. Princesses did not marry cowboys. Not for real. Especially not a princess who had to find a husband listed in the top third of *Forbes* five hundred richest men.

She studied Buck's rugged profile. He was the first person who'd trusted her to do anything. He'd known all along that she was a princess, yet it didn't seem to matter. He liked her, even if all she did was rake manure or wash dishes. He didn't want her crown.

Suddenly she was absolutely certain that this was the man she wanted to spend the rest of her life with, the one she wanted to wake up with every morning, the one she wanted to have children with.

But she couldn't.

Her eyes dropped to his soft cotton shirt with a tear in the sleeve and his frayed pair of jeans. He was poor. A man who lived from paycheck to paycheck. And she needed a husband who was rich. Very, very rich.

If she didn't find one soon, Bonifay would sell her—and Montclaire—to the highest bidder.

Josie turned her head to hide the tears stinging her eyes.

The years ahead seemed like a bottomless black hole. She'd never again hear his voice calling her sweetheart, never see his blue eyes watching her like a man with a sweet tooth eyes a dessert tray, never inhale the unique odor that would let her recognize him even if she lost all her other senses.

She dug her fingernails into her palms to help her fight the tears.

She'd known that life wasn't fair from the first moment she'd realized what it meant to be a princess. But this...

As Melissa would so colorfully put it—this sucked Gravy Train.

Buck was worried. They'd been driving for over an hour, and already he'd barely avoided a state trooper, a small-town cop and what was possibly a roadblock.

Not only did whoever was looking for them know he had Princess Joséphene, they knew where he was going. Like a fox going to ground, he was trying to make a run for his lair, driving north toward the Double Star. There was a re-mote cabin back in the hills that he'd hoped to hide in, but now he had to change his plans.

He was headed north on Highway 49. In just a few miles, Highway 16 split off from it. They would expect him to follow Highway 49 north toward the Double Star. They'd probably be covering Highway 16, too, but not as thor-oughly. So, that's the way he was heading.

He had to make some arrangements first, and the only way to do that was on his cell phone. As soon as he hit Send, the FBI would be able to pinpoint his location, but that was okay as long as he was still on Forty-Nine when he used it.

Hoping the phone wouldn't be too hard to explain to Jo-sie, he reached into the glove compartment and pulled it out. He pressed Power and checked the battery. It was pow-ered up.

"You have a cell phone?" she asked right on cue. "Why haven't I seen it before?"

He didn't ask how she'd thought they were logging onto the Internet. He'd been careful not to let her watch when he set up the computer, draping the phone wire over the other side of the table with the power cord and hiding the phone under a towel. "I keep it for emergencies."

She accepted his explanation with a frown. "Who are you calling?"

"A...uh, buddy of mine. We need some help if we're going to lose them."

Her first reaction was to turn and look out the back window. But of course the trailer blocked her view. "Are we being followed?"

He keyed in the number of his ranch foreman, who always carried a cell phone so Buck could keep in touch. "No, but they know where we're headed."

"Where?"

He was surprised she hadn't asked earlier. "We're headed north. We were going to a little cabin I know about. Now we've got to change our plans without seeming to."

"How are we going to accomplish that?"

He'd already pushed the Send button. "I'll explain in a minute."

Cleve Tyler answered on the second ring. "Tyler."

"What's up, Cleve?"

"Hellfire, son. What are you doing calling me? Don't you know they'll be on you like flies on cow patties?"

"I take it the FBI has come calling?"

"They've been crawling all over the ranch like ants at a picnic. Your mama's here, too. She's been driving me up a wall, wanting to know where you're at. I've been out checking fences all day just to get away from the ruckus. What the hell you been up to? And who's this princess they've been jabbering about?"

Buck smiled. "My wife."

"Your wife! Hell and damnation, son. You went and married a princess? After all your mama's put you through?"

"'Fraid so."

After a small hesitation during which Buck could almost hear his grandfather's old friend shaking his head, Cleve asked curiously, "An honest-to-God princess?"

"An honest-to-God princess."

"Well, hell. I reckon you know what you're doing. And I reckon you didn't call just to chat. What you need?"

"I need a decoy, Cleve."

"A decoy, huh?"

"Seth Capshaw still have that little Mexican girlfriend?"

"Bonita? Yeah."

"And that old Ford truck?"

"Yeah. Ain't much to look at, but he keeps it running like a top."

"Good. I need him to meet me and switch trucks. He'll drive mine back to the ranch, and I'll take his and head in a different direction."

"Where you want him to meet you at?"

"Oroville. You know that truck stop just off Seventy?"

"Yep."

"We should be there in a couple of hours. Maybe two-and-a-half. He needs to bring his girlfriend. Tell him to gas up his truck, then meet us in the rest rooms. We'll exchange clothes and keys and head out. Got that?"

"Got it. Seth's working not too far away. I'll send him on as soon as I can find him. Good luck."

"Thanks." Buck pressed End and glanced at Josie. "Any questions?"

"Where are we going after we switch trucks?"

"I figure we'll head over to the coast. We can hole up in a beach house I know of for a while."

The simple house belonged to his attorney and the only friend he kept up with from high school, Howard Moore, who occasionally liked to get away from it all. Luckily, Buck knew where he kept the spare keys.

"I guess we won't have the camper," she said.

"No. Seth'll take Aggie back to the ranch."

"What ranch?"

Buck could have kicked himself for the slip, but he covered it quickly. "The one where Cleve works."

"Won't a beach house be expensive?"

He shook his head. "It belongs to a friend. It's not fancy, but he won't mind us using it for a while."

"Who cares about fancy? If we can just stay to the twenty-eighth, then I won't have to hide any longer."

"What happens on May twenty-eighth?"

"It's the day after my twenty-fifth birthday."

Since Montclaire's obscure law wasn't common knowledge, he had to play along. "Do you turn into a pumpkin or something?"

The ring of the cell phone startled them both.

"Damn," Buck said. "Why the hell didn't I turn this thing off?"

"Aren't you going to answer it?" she asked when he hadn't picked it up after two rings.

He cussed again. No telling who it was, but it might be Cleve, calling with some question or problem. He had to answer it.

He snatched it up and pressed Send. "Yeah?"

"Hardin?"

He barely suppressed a groan. "Mother."

"Good gracious, Hardin, where have you been? I've been trying to contact you for a week! Your phone was either busy or off."

"I know. That was on purpose." He glanced at Josie, who watched him quizzically.

"Have you talked to the FBI yet, son?"

"No, Mother. And I won't, if I have anything to say about it."

"Well, good for you, son. They're the most obnoxious people I've ever met. Your father and I keep telling them you wouldn't kidnap a princess, but they simply won't believe me."

"I'm sorry you had to go through that, Mother, but I have to go. I need to stay off the line." It was just a few more miles to the turn.

"Is it true?" she asked breathlessly.

He rolled his eyes. "Is what true?"

"Have you married Princess Joséphene of Montclaire?"

He debated what to tell her, but decided she probably already knew the truth and lying wouldn't help him. "Yes and no."

"What does that mean?"

"Yes, we're married, but we're not staying that way."

"Why not? Don't tell me you've still got on those old boots and jeans."

"Yep."

She groaned. "With a princess? No wonder she wants to divorce you so quickly. You didn't kidnap her, did you? Tell me that's not true."

"No, Mother. She was perfectly willing. Listen, it's complicated and I need to go. Do me a favor, will you?"

"What?"

"Are you there by the answering machine?"

"Yes, Hardin."

"Good. Press Record. I'm going to put Jo— the princess on the line so she can talk and assure the FBI she's with me of her own free will and doesn't want them trying to find us. Okay? Did you do it?"

"It's recording, Hardin. Am I really going to speak to the princess?"

"Yes, Mother. Here."

He took the phone away from his ear. "You up for this? It might help."

Josie twisted her mouth wryly. "I doubt it. Bonifay's too persistent. But we can try."

He handed her the phone.

"Hello?" she said into it. "Yes, this is really Princess

Joséphene.... Nice to meet you, Mrs. Buchanan. You have a warm, generous son.... Yes, we're really married.... In Reno, last Friday night. No, I guess it was early Saturday morning, about two o'clock.''

Buck cast more glances at Josie than the road. She'd changed into another woman right before his eyes. A princess—with ramrod-straight posture and the same high-toned voice his mother used. Only...

He'd gotten to know Josie before Joséphene, so he knew what lay beneath the surface. With his mother, he'd never attempted to find out.

Uncomfortable with that insight, he shifted on the seat. "Get to the important part. We need to turn the phone off."

"All right, Mrs. Buchanan.... I just want to say that I'm married to Hardin Buchanan, also known as Buck Buchanan. I married him of my own volition. We are on our honeymoon and do not want to be disturbed. Please call off the search. I'm fine. I'm happy. I just want to be alone with my husband. That's all."

Buck reached for the phone. "You need to hang up now."

"The Christmas Ball? Yes, Mrs. Buchanan, I've heard my friend Melissa Porter talk about it." She met Buck's gaze. "Attend this year?"

He shook his head vehemently. "Hang up."

"We'll have to discuss that later, I'm afraid. Buck says I need to go.... Yes. Thank you. Goodbye."

She handed him the phone, and he pressed Power to turn it off.

"So that's your mother," Josie said.

He glanced at her, then back to the road. "Yeah."

"She's not what I thought she'd be."

"Yeah? How's that?"

"I don't know. Like you. She sounded sophisticated, educated."

"I don't sound ed-ji-cated?"

She didn't take the bait. "Are you?"

He glanced out the driver's-side mirror to hide his frown. If he told her about his advanced degree from the number-one business school in the nation, she'd start asking a lot of other questions he didn't want to answer. "I graduated high school."

She took so long to comment on his reply that he looked over to see her studying him speculatively—as if she was beginning to piece together all the inconsistencies. Better distract her. Quick.

"So what's the problem with your country?"

She took the bait. With a sigh, she faced forward again. "Montclaire's economy is in shambles. While Bonifay has been at the helm, the world has been passing us by. The infrastructure is so antiquated, modern technology is virtually impossible. We need an influx of cash, and soon, if we are not to go bankrupt."

"Ever thought of a bank?"

"I talked with one of Mr. Porter's banker friends. He said we'd be extremely lucky to find a bank that would give us as much money as we need when we have someone like Bonifay running things."

Unable to help himself, Buck asked questions about the small country—population statistics, gross national product, exports and imports. Questions whose answers would give him a picture about the health of Montclaire's economy.

Her replies intrigued him.

The principality had two valuable products to offer the world—marble and tourism. Neither had to be exploited so much it ruined the old-world charm of the island country, but between the two, they could bring the economy around.

Buck could do the same for Montclaire that he'd done for all the small companies he'd—

Damn. Was he actually considering investing in Montclaire?

What would he do, tell the world he'd give Montclaire the capital they needed, but he didn't want their princess? That he'd given her a trial period as his wife and she hadn't lived up to snuff?

He couldn't humiliate Josie that way, which meant he couldn't invest in Montclaire without staying married to her. And he couldn't stay married without ruining his own plans.

All he wanted was a simple life—running the Double Star in peace, and investing on the side. He certainly didn't want to be Prince of Montclaire. Or Prince Consort. Or whatever the hell title they'd give him.

The title "Cowboy" was more than enough for him.

Chapter Nine

"Josie? Wake up, sweetheart. We're here."

Josie slowly roused herself from her warm, comfortable nest against Buck's shoulder. "What time is it?"

"Well after midnight."

Suddenly her senses came awake and a feeling of homecoming swamped her sleepy brain. She could hear waves crashing against a not-too-distant shore, and the familiar smell of warm, salty air wafted through Buck's open window.

She sat up. With no light but starlight anywhere around, the night was as black as the depths of the ocean. She could barely make out the faint outline of a small house. "Where are we?"

They'd stopped in Oroville just after dark and switched trucks with Seth and his girlfriend without incident. Buck had instructed Josie to talk with Seth's girlfriend as little as possible in case there was anyone listening, but the young woman had watched Josie with worshipful eyes.

As a princess, Josie was accustomed to such adulation.

Accustomed, but never comfortable with it. Josie's only claim to fame was that she was a princess. Why should she be loved for something so meaningless?

The undeserved worship had always bothered her, but tonight she'd felt it more acutely than she had in the past. Maybe because she'd had a week during which no one had regarded her with anything other than mild interest in another human being.

She had Buck to thank for that.

As she thought his name, he opened his door. "On the coast. Does it really matter where?"

Josie blinked when the open door triggered the overhead light. Though weak, it glared against the almost total darkness. "I guess not. I probably wouldn't know the name of the town, anyway."

"What town? We're miles from anywhere. That's one reason we're here."

"Whose house is this again?"

"It belongs to a friend. He won't mind us using it, and I know where he keeps a key."

Since Buck held the door open and she was as close to it as she was to the other one, she scooted under the wheel.

He held out his hand to help her down.

She hesitated. It wasn't that the gesture was unfamiliar. How many times had an impersonal hand been extended to assist Princess Joséphene as she alighted from a limousine or carriage?

However, this was something Buck had never done. If he'd helped her out of the truck at all during the past week, it was always with both hands around her waist.

She lifted her gaze to his. The shadows cast by the weak overhead light made him look tired, haggard.

"What?" he demanded impatiently. "Isn't the house up to your royal standards?"

This was exactly what she'd been afraid of ever since

she'd found out he knew she was a princess. Now that it was out in the open, he was going to treat her like one.

"I haven't even seen it yet," she said. "If your trailer was good enough for me, why wouldn't this house be good enough?"

His face seemed to relax, though he didn't smile. "Come on. I'd like to get a little sleep tonight."

He stepped closer and wrapped his large hands around her waist to lift her down.

Josie's feet stung when they hit the ground, but she didn't mind. In fact, she smiled.

"What now?" He kept his hands around her waist and didn't step back.

She leaned into him. "You're not going to treat me like a princess now, are you?"

"Do you want me to?"

"No!"

He gave her a tired smile and shifted subtly to fit their bodies together. "Good. I'd hate to give up my own personal chef and laundress."

Josie rubbed her hands up his cotton-covered biceps. "You've done so much for me. Cooking and cleaning for you is the least I can do. And I like helping you. I really do."

He leaned down as if to kiss her, but instead he placed his forehead against hers. "I know. I think you're crazy, but I know."

Though disappointed that he didn't kiss her, Josie closed her eyes and reveled in the embrace. The warm, strong arms of the man she loved were wrapped around her, and his breath mingled with hers. Being held this way made her feel safe, protected, loved.

Did the feeling come from her imagination, or did he love her?

The possibility made her breath catch.

It would be much, much better if he didn't. That way, only one of them would be torn apart when she left.

"Come on, sweetheart." He drew away, but took her hand in his. "Let's get the key."

Buck turned off the noon news with a frown. The search for Princess Joséphene was intensifying. The media was caught up in the frenzy, playing Josie's taped message again and again, with "experts" analyzing every word, every inflection—had she been kidnapped and forced to marry, or did she marry Hardin Buchanan of her own free will?

They produced a copy of Buck and Josie's marriage license and interviewed the justice of the peace in Reno who'd married them.

A redheaded young woman named Melissa Porter Denton—who was identified as Josie's friend—looked straight into the cameras and told the world to get off Josie's case.

They'd questioned Buck's parents and had dug up all kinds of statistics on him, including his last tax return.

Thank God Josie had begged off watching the news with him.

Prince Henri had even taped a message, offering one million American dollars—to anyone—for his daughter's safe return.

If the FBI didn't find them, some greedy bounty hunter would. It was only a matter of time now. Days. Maybe hours.

He stood abruptly from the overstuffed red leather couch in the beach house's living room, frustration running so deep he felt eaten up with it. Yes, she was getting to him, but he'd give away every last cent in every bank account for just a little more time with her.

His ambivalence slapped him in the face. He wanted her, but didn't want to stay married to her. How selfish could he be?

In an attempt to escape his thoughts, he walked around the couch to the French doors leading out onto the porch that overlooked the ocean. Josie stood on the edge of the cliff a hundred yards away, gazing up the coast.

He could have forever with her, if he wanted it. All he had to do was what he ached to do anyway—make love to her.

He knew that much of his frustration stemmed from his self-imposed celibacy. He wanted Josie more than he'd ever wanted anything in his life. But to have her, he had to give up the life he wanted.

He smiled bitterly. He was willing to give up hundreds of millions of dollars to have her—but not being a cowboy.

Or was he?

Despite his efforts to shove away the thoughts when they surfaced, he'd given a lot of thought to investing in Montclaire. The possibilities intrigued him as no investment had in quite a while. Not only was the potential for personal profit enormous, he'd be bolstering the island's economy by providing jobs for its people and bringing in a steady flow of capital. It was a win-win situation.

He knew that if he'd heard about the opportunity before he'd married Josie, he'd have jumped on it with his bankbook blazing.

Now there were too many strings attached.

Strings, hell. More like chains that would trap him forever in the kind of life he swore he'd never live.

Then again—he'd have Josie.

What a choice. He could either have the woman he wanted and a life he hated, or the life he wanted without the woman he loved.

His thoughts came to a screeching halt.

The woman he loved.

He'd been fighting his passion for her so long, he didn't realize she'd sneaked into his heart.

Now the question was—which did he want worse? The life he loved or the woman he loved?

Unable to answer the question, he shoved past the French doors. He needed something to occupy his mind, and he knew Josie was the only thing that would satisfy him at the moment. If he couldn't have her body, at least he could have her company.

He strode across a yard the length of a football field. The house had been built this far from the cliff so it wouldn't be destroyed if the cliff eroded in a bad storm or collapsed in an earthquake.

Josie stood with legs slightly apart, braced against the breeze that molded her shirt to her body and lifted strands of her hair like dark flags. She couldn't possibly have heard his approach over the pounding of the surf below. Still, she turned to smile at him when he was about twenty yards away. Her expression made him ache with longing. He'd waited all his life for a woman to look at him this way.

Her amber eyes were luminous, full of...could it be love?

Far from alarming him, the possibility made something unravel inside Buck—like a knot around his heart that he didn't know existed. Freed, his heart expanded to crowd his lungs, making it hard to breathe.

He stopped a few feet short of her, knowing that if he didn't, he'd kiss her. He wanted to taste her more than he ever wanted to see another cow.

That realization *did* alarm him, and he clenched his hands at his sides to keep from reaching for her.

The next thing he knew she was waving a hand in front of his face. "Hellooo? Buck? Are you in there?"

He blinked. "What?"

She chuckled. "You *are* alive."

He shook his head to clear it. "You say something?"

"I asked what they said on the news."

Buck forced himself to relax. At least enough to answer

her question. "About what we expected. They played your message and analyzed it to death. They interviewed my parents and the guy who married us. And some woman named Melissa Denton. A friend?"

She nodded.

"Oh, and your father made a passionate appeal to me not to hurt you."

Her smile faded. "Passionate? My father?"

"He wants his daughter to come home. All is forgiven…etcetera."

"What did Bonifay have to say?"

"Come to think of it, there wasn't anything about him."

Her frown deepened. "Are you sure? It's not like him to lose an opportunity for international exposure."

"I didn't hear his name mentioned even once."

"Interesting." Her gaze shifted out to sea.

He wanted her attention here with him, so he grabbed her hand. "Let's walk on the beach."

Her face cleared, and she smiled. "How do we get down there?"

He led her carefully down the steps cut into the side of the cliff. They took off their shoes and meandered along the beach for over an hour. Buck asked Josie details about her life. Freed from having to lie, she talked openly. What she said made his heart ache for the little girl who had no mother and virtually no father. Her only true friend, it seemed, was this Melissa Porter—now Denton.

When their walk was cut short by a high rock wall, they sat on the sand, just out of reach of the waves.

"How long do you think it'll be before they find us?" Josie asked after a comfortable silence.

He wanted her to think they had all the time in the world, so she wouldn't worry. "We're pretty isolated here, and no one saw us come in."

"That we know of."

Why did he even try? She was too smart to be fooled.

"One thing I didn't tell you. Your father is offering a reward for your return. One million dollars."

"Montclaire doesn't have that much money." Josie shook her head. "So how long do we have?"

He shrugged. "A few days, maybe, before someone will make the connection between me and Howie."

"Howie?"

"The guy who owns the house."

"What does he do? Is he a rodeo cowboy like you?"

"No." Buck frowned. He was tired of lying, too. "He's a lawyer."

"A lawyer?" Surprise was clear in her voice.

Buck nodded. "An old high-school friend."

"Oh."

Several moments of thoughtful silence were broken when Josie said, "Buck?"

"Yeah?"

"I know we've had this discussion before, but..." She sighed heavily. "Would you please, *please* make love to me?"

Her words were bullets slamming into his gut. It took a moment for him to draw enough air to reply. "No."

"Why?" Her voice was small, plaintive. "Don't you want me?"

"I want you more than I've ever wanted anything in my life."

"Then why?"

"You're a virgin."

Her hands struck the sand and her fingers dug in. "You keep bringing that up, as if it matters."

"It matters. Believe me."

"Yes. It matters because if I'm still a virgin by the time they find us, they'll annul our marriage and make me marry Alphonse Picquet. You don't know him, but he's a sadistic, rapacious man who'll ruin Montclaire. And..." Her voice broke. "...and he won't be very nice to me."

The thought of Josie clamped in Picquet's sweaty embrace made Buck want to ram his fists into the nearest rock.

"It's not only that," she added softly. "I want you, Buck. I want my first time to be with you."

His will nearly broke. He almost reached for her. Only strength of will kept him from an act that might ruin both their lives forever. "I'm sorry, Josie. You're a princess and I'm just a simple cowboy. You aren't for the likes of me."

"That's for me to decide, isn't it?"

"What if they make us stay married? What if there's some law in your country that says you can't get divorced?"

"If Princess Diana could get a divorce, so can I."

He shook his head. "I can't take that chance. I'd never survive in your world. I'd hate it. Then I might begin to hate you, and that wouldn't be pleasant for either of us."

She was silent so long, he chanced a glance at her. She looked unblinkingly out to sea, tears brimming in her eyes.

Her tears tore him in two.

No! He couldn't give in now, not after fighting the temptation this long. "Josie, I'm sorry."

She shrugged stiffly. "It's not your fault I was born a princess."

"I wish I could—"

"Please. Don't say anything more. I'm sorry I mentioned it again. I'm sorry I—" Suddenly the dam of tears broke. With a sob, she leaped to her feet and ran down the beach.

Buck grabbed handfuls of sand to force himself to stay down. He fought the overwhelming impulse to follow her, to apologize, to make love to her for the next hundred years.

But he couldn't. He had to be strong—for both their sakes. If he stayed with her, he'd be miserable and eventually he'd make her miserable, too.

He wearily rubbed a hand down his face, welcoming the grains of sand that dug into his skin.

As if he hadn't already made her miserable.

As if he wasn't miserable. As if he wasn't going to be miserable for the rest of his life if he didn't have her.

But he'd also be miserable living the way his parents did.

He thought about how ecstatic his mother had been to learn he'd married Princess Joséphene. He'd done exactly the opposite of what he'd intended to do. He'd wanted to find a trailer-park queen to get his parents off his back. Instead, he'd fulfilled their wildest dreams.

Buck frowned as those thoughts caught in his mind.

He was wrong. Getting his parents off his back was only a small part of the reason he'd wanted to marry a trailer-park queen. Mainly, he'd wanted to irritate them. To show them they couldn't control him.

His frown deepened.

Was he really basing his future happiness on what would irritate his parents?

Suddenly he realized it was what he'd been doing his whole life. It was one of the main reasons he'd chosen to be a cowboy, even though what really interested him—investing—didn't fit into the cowboy life-style.

But then, he didn't fit into either life-style—his parents' or his grandfather's. He was a half-breed, not truly comfortable or fully accepted by the people in either world.

Josie accepted all of him. To her, it didn't matter whether he was a cowboy who played the stock market or an investor who played cowboy. She wanted both sides of him. She understood him because she lived two separate lives, just like he did.

Humbled, Buck realized for the first time exactly what he'd be giving up if he said goodbye to Josie. The chance to become whole. The chance to live with someone who loved both sides of him.

But could he be happy living as the husband of a princess?

Hell, he didn't know. All he knew is that he wouldn't be happy without her.

True, there'd be times when he'd have to endure the social world he hated. But with Josie holding his hand, he could put up with anything. Together, they'd have the strength to do what they hadn't been able to do separately— live the lives they wanted to live. Be who they wanted to be.

He looked down the line of footprints in the sand. Their footprints, side by side, continuing as far as he could see.

Suddenly he knew that as long as he had Josie walking beside him, he could tolerate anything. Without her, he'd never be happy.

So what if the world sometimes got in the way? He'd smile at the world and wave—just like Josie had been doing all her life. She'd be there to teach him how.

Buck rose to his feet with a smile. He was going back to the beach house and making love to his wife. He wasn't going to let her out of bed until the posse came banging on the door.

Josie had stopped crying by the time she reached the steps up the cliff. Crying wasn't going to help.

The trouble was, nothing would. She'd found the only man she could ever love, and he didn't want her because of who she was.

She would have laughed if she hadn't been so busy fighting tears. She hated being loved just because she was a princess. And now she'd discovered she hated *not* being loved just because she was a princess.

But how could she blame Buck? She felt exactly the same way. She hated being a princess, but she couldn't walk away from it as easily as he could. She'd been born a princess and would remain one until she died.

Zut!

If she had to dedicate her life to Montclaire, why couldn't she have this one consolation? Was having the man she loved asking too much?

She knew the answer as soon as the question formed in her mind. She'd known from the beginning that she couldn't have Buck. They'd both agreed their marriage was temporary. He wasn't rich enough for her, and she lived a lifestyle he hated.

The problem was, she'd fallen in love with her temporary husband, and she didn't know if she had the strength to endure a life without him.

The clock read ten to four when she reached the house. Not yet time to start dinner. She had no idea when Buck would return. She hoped he'd stay away for several hours. She needed to collect herself, to marshal her inner defenses so she could be the charming companion he deserved for the rest of the time they had together.

She could do it. She'd had lots of practice smiling when all she wanted to do was scream.

Remembering the beach house's one nod to luxury—a whirlpool bath—she decided a nice, long soak would help.

After twisting up her hair, she turned on the water in the tub, then removed her secondhand clothes and Wal-Mart underwear. Since the tub was large, it took a while to fill, so she sat on the edge and stared at the water level rising.

When tears began to sting her eyes, she fought them until they went away. Tears only made her eyes puffy. They didn't solve any—

A movement in the mirrored wall behind the tub caught her attention. She glanced up—and froze.

Buck stood in the doorway, staring at her with eyes that

were on fire. His heated gaze traveled over every inch of her nakedness.

Josie didn't move, didn't try to hide her body from his intent perusal. As he looked, she felt the muscles in her stomach tighten and her nipples contract to nubs.

"Josie," he uttered in a choked whisper.

"Buck," she breathed. "What...?"

His gaze rose and met hers in the mirror. "You're beautiful."

"What are you doing here?"

"I want you," he said simply.

"But you said—"

"To hell with what I said." He stepped slowly toward her. "You're my wife. I've wanted you from the instant I saw you in that tacky rodeo-princess outfit. I can't stand it any longer."

When he reached the side of the tub, he stood at her back. The rough heat of his jeans pressing against her matched the velvet heat of the water swirling around her calves, making goose bumps dance over the skin in between.

"They won't make us stay married, Buck," she assured him. "Bonifay will take one look at your bank account and insist on a divorce."

"We'll talk about that later." Bending slowly, he slid his hands down her arms. "Right now, I've got my wife on my mind."

Josie didn't care if they waited to talk about it until the sky collapsed. Buck's hands had taken a detour at her elbow, following instead the curve of her hips. She leaned back against him, her heartbeat drowning out the sound of the running water.

"Do you like to feel my hands on your skin?" he breathed into her ear.

"Yes." Frustrated at not having any of him to touch, she

lifted her arms and wrapped them around his neck. "Please don't stop this time."

He chuckled softly. "I won't, sweetheart. I love touching you. I'm going to touch every inch of you." He pressed a kiss on her nape, making her gasp at the sharp stab of pleasure. "In one way or another."

His hands rubbed their way down the outside of her thighs, then trailed up the inside.

Josie's hips arched to hurry the ascent, but he avoided the throbbing place that ached for the pressure of his touch, gently kneading her stomach instead. "Buck, please."

He nibbled his way across her shoulder. "You don't want that yet."

"Yes, I do!"

He smiled against her skin. "No. There are other places that need attention first."

"Like what?"

He lifted his hands to cup her breasts. "Like these."

Air rushed into Josie's lungs so quickly, she felt as if she would faint. Fire burned in her brain, scorching away every thought but getting closer to the hands driving pleasure into every cell in her body.

"Buck?"

"Yes?"

"I want you."

"I know, sweet Josie. I want you, too."

"Now."

"Patience. Aren't you enjoying me touching you?"

"Yes, but—" She moaned as he gently plucked at her nipples.

"But what?"

"I want to touch you, too."

"Don't worry, sweetheart. We have plenty of time for that. Right now, I'm having a good time watching you as I touch you."

She opened her eyes to find him watching her reaction to his hands on her body. When she looked, she couldn't believe the woman in the mirror was her. The dark-haired woman with slumberous eyes looked nothing like a princess. She looked like a very sexy woman, writhing with every touch from her man.

That was the woman she wanted to be. The woman she was—with Buck.

"I love you," she whispered, unable to stop the words. But she didn't care. She wanted him to know.

His arms tightened around her and his hands stilled. He drew a long, shuddering breath, then uttered, "Josie?"

"Yes?"

"Turn off the water."

He didn't hold her back, but his touch never left her as she leaned forward and twisted the knobs. As soon as the water shut off, he stood and scooped her into his arms.

She gasped and wrapped her arms around his neck. "Where are we going?"

"To bed." He nibbled on her neck as he carried her into the bedroom. "It's time you officially became Mrs. Buck Buchanan."

Chapter Ten

Buck woke to a warm feeling of bone-deep satisfaction.

He instantly knew why.

Josie lay curled against him. He could feel her velvet skin on his—from the naked back pressing into his chest, down to the heels against his shins. One of his arms was draped over her hip, the other formed her pillow.

With every breath he inhaled her soft scent. She smelled of salt air and sex. A helluva lot more fragrant than a herd of cows.

He smiled against her black hair, remembering the last few hours. Their wedding night—at last.

He'd spent over an hour preparing her to lose her virginity. So long, in fact, that she barely noticed when he entered her body for the first time.

His little princess had definitely been a surprise. She'd eagerly followed wherever he led. She matched him kiss for kiss, touch for touch, thrust for thrust.

His own body tightened at the memory of being inside her, but he fought arousal. He wasn't going to make love to her again until he'd told her who he was, until she understood there would be no divorce.

Probably not even then. Though he'd eased her initiation into womanhood, she was bound to be sore.

They had forever. He could wait a day or two before having her again.

Buck looked over his shoulder at the clock on the bedside table. Dusk had been falling as they'd drifted off to sleep. Now the room was nearly as dark as Josie's hair.

Nine-fifteen. Early enough to wake her.

He switched on the lamp, then let the hand on her hip dip down to her stomach. He hadn't used protection. They might have already begun a new life.

The possibility made something primal swell in his heart. Pure male vanity. He hadn't considered it before, but now he found he wanted to make Josie pregnant. He wanted to see her growing big with his child.

He was going to make starting a family his number-one priority.

He felt another part of him swell at the notion, but he ignored it. First he had to tell Josie he'd been…misleading her about his financial situation, and he didn't know how she was going to take it.

Then again, she couldn't very well cast stones when she was guilty of mendacity as well.

"Josie? Wake up, sweetheart."

He watched her wake in stages—going from irritation to confusion to alarm. Her last emotion, thank God, was delight. When she realized who she was in bed with, she twisted toward him with a happy smile. "Hello."

She looked so sexy waking up from exhaustion induced by his lovemaking, he had to kiss her. "Hello, yourself."

"Mmm. What time is it?"

"A little after nine."

She watched her finger run down his unshaven jaw.

"What does one say after...such an experience? I've had etiquette from all parts of the world drilled into my head, but none of it seems to fit the situation."

He chuckled. "The boarding school didn't teach you bedroom manners? Not a complete education for a princess. We'll have to home-school our daughter, if we have one."

Her smile faded. "Buck..."

"What happened to *I love you*?"

She glanced up. "What?"

"That seems like an appropriate thing to say after you've been loved to exhaustion."

She relaxed. "I do, you know."

"Do you?"

She nodded, but didn't look happy about it.

"Then say the words," he whispered.

She frowned. "I shouldn't love you. I won't be allowed to keep you."

He pushed a strand of black hair off her cheek. "Say it."

When her eyes met his they told him more eloquently than words ever could, but still she repeated them. "I love you."

"And I—"

A loud crash from the living room tore the words from his throat. He bolted up but didn't have time to stand before four heavily armed men in black swarmed into the room.

"*Mon Dieu,*" Josie whispered from her protected place against his back.

"It's all right, Josie. They won't—"

Before he could finish, two men grabbed him and threw him facedown on the floor. They twisted his arms around to his back. One knelt on him while the other fastened handcuffs around his wrists.

"What the hell are you doing?" he demanded. "Who are you?"

"The ones dragging your butt down to the FBI."

"Bounty hunters," Buck spat.

"Stop this instant!" Josie grabbed a pillow and began pummeling the man kneeling on Buck. "I demand you let my husband go."

From his position on the floor, he caught a glimpse of a naked breast as she attacked. "Josie, cover yourself!"

She snatched the sheet up, then struck a princess pose on the bed. "Who's in charge here?"

A man standing over Buck said, "What's it to you?"

Josie's chin lifted. "Release my husband immediately."

Now that they had him cuffed, Buck's captors hauled him to his feet.

"How did you find us?" Buck demanded.

Josie began stepping off the bed, but the man on the other side grabbed her arm.

"Police scanners are dandy little things. Give you all sorts of information. Like overhearing a boater outta Rockport who spotted the lights on here and knew they shouldn't be. We made the connection and made sure we got here before the police."

"Keep your dirty hands off her!" Buck struggled against the cuffs, but was held in place by the men on either side of him. He glared at the leader. "Do you know who I am?"

The man stared back at him with dead black eyes. "You look enough like the picture I saw of Hardin Buchanan to pass."

"I'll give you two million dollars to let us go right now."

"Buck!" Josie's voice was horrified. "You don't have that much money."

The man looked between them with narrow eyes, obviously weighing the possibilities. Finally, he made the decision. "Take him out."

Buck held firm against the hands tugging on him. "You're going to give up doubling your reward?"

"No hard feelings. Just playing it safe. A million dollars in the hand is worth two in the bush."

Buck's captors dragged him backward.

"Stop!" Again Josie was restrained from reaching him. "Please stop!"

The stony-faced men paid her no heed. They dragged Buck away as if they never heard her.

Buck twisted at the door. "Don't worry, sweetheart. We'll get this straightened out."

"Buck! No!" She struck at the man holding her.

Buck memorized the guy's face, vowing to put a fist through it if he ever saw it again.

"At least let him put on some clothes," she said angrily.

The leader shrugged. "Don't worry, lady. The FBI will put pants on him when he reaches Sacramento."

The men tugged on Buck. "Come on."

Buck met Josie's eyes. "I'll see you in a few hours."

"I love you!" she cried.

Then he was jerked from the room.

"May I come in, Princess Joséphene?"

Josie turned from the hotel window where dawn was creeping over Sacramento. The low but heavily accented voice came from a woman standing at the door of the suite's bedroom.

"Who are you?" The question was rude, but at the moment Josie didn't care. Somewhere in this wretched American city Buck was being questioned by the FBI, and no one would tell her where.

The woman who looked to be in her mid-thirties replied in French. "My name is Madame Sophie Angousset. I have come at your father's request to make sure you are taken safely home. I'm sorry I wasn't here when you arrived. I was making arrangements for our return."

Josie's chin lifted and she replied in English. "I'm not

going home until I see my husband. And don't try to wrap something foul in clean linen. I know who runs Montclaire. Prime Minister Bonifay sent you, not my father.''

Madame Angousset stepped into the room, but stayed a respectful distance away. She was a few inches shorter than Josie, with intelligent green eyes and auburn hair swept back into an elegant twist.

She smiled serenely. "No, your father sent me. Many things have changed since you disappeared."

Part of Josie wanted to follow that line of conversation, but she was too distracted. "Where's my husband?"

Madame Angousset spread her hands. "I'm sorry. I don't know."

"I see." Josie turned back to the window. For the first time, she could understand her father losing himself in grief. "You're just another dragon like Madame Savoie. A keeper for the princess."

"I was born on Montclaire but married a Frenchman and lived with him in Provence. He died three years ago, but I remained in France." She gave an eloquent Gallic shrug. "When I was at home last week visiting my parents, I met your father, and he asked me to be your companion."

"You mean Bonifay offered you the job."

"No. It was Prince Henri."

Josie regarded her skeptically. "My father has barely been aware he has a country since my mother died."

"Things have changed. When you disappeared and Prince Henri thought he was going to lose you, too, he snapped out of his grief. He stripped Bonifay of his power. Your father is once again ruling Montclaire. He's the one who's been dealing with the authorities searching for you."

Josie dropped into the nearest chair. "My disappearance woke him?"

"Indeed, yes."

Josie didn't know what to think. She had no inkling she meant so much to her father. "Is he in the United States?"

Madame Angousset shook her head. "He was afraid Bonifay might try to regain power, so he felt he had to remain on Montclaire. But he's been speaking to the president here daily."

"I can't believe this. Perhaps I should've eloped years ago."

The older woman smiled. "I know you've had a difficult night, but do you think you could manage to call your father before you rest? He's most anxious to assure himself that you've come to no harm."

Josie's eyes found the phone next to the bed. Talk to her father? It was what she'd wanted to do all her life. Yet the concept was so foreign to her, she couldn't imagine what to say to him. She'd dined with the man every day of her adult life, except for when she'd been sent abroad to make a state appearance or had been given Bonifay's rare permission to take her thoroughbreds to a horse show. But she didn't know him.

With heart pounding, she watched as the older woman contacted the hotel operator. A few minutes later, Madame Angousset's face changed subtly. She looked and sounded as if she were speaking to an angel, though her words were formal.

Suddenly, Josie's attention was caught by the word *chéri*.

The endearment startled her. Was there a romantic liaison between her father and Madame Angousset? Had her father forgotten her mother so quickly?

The woman turned to her with a smile. "Your father is anxious to speak with you, Princess."

Josie blinked away her surprise. Twenty years was not quick. Perhaps Madame Angousset had given her father further reason to break through his shell. If so, Josie could only be grateful. And, somehow, knowing Madame Angousset felt the same way about her father that she felt about Buck made her seem more like a woman than a dragon.

Josie stood and walked to the desk, taking the phone from Madame Angousset's hands. "Hello? Papa?"

"Minette."

Josie almost dropped the phone at the once-familiar endearment. Her father hadn't called her "kitten" since the day her mother died.

"Are you all right?" he asked anxiously.

"Yes, Papa. I'm fine. I didn't need to be rescued."

"Why didn't you call me and let me know you were alive?"

"I didn't know..." How could she tell her father she didn't call because she believed he wouldn't care? "I thought Bonifay..."

"I deposed Bonifay within hours of your disappearance. Didn't Mr. Buchanan let you see the news?"

"I didn't want to, Papa. The media don't know the true facts half the time. The other half, they lie."

A brief silence ensued. Finally her father sighed. "It's good to hear your voice, Joséphene. It seems like a long time since I've heard it." His voice broke. He cleared his throat, obviously pulling himself together. "I know I haven't been the best father."

"Papa, it doesn't matter."

"Yes, it does matter. I've failed you, and I've failed Montclaire. But those days are past. I've been trapped in a thick fog for nearly twenty years, trying to find my way out. But it's finally clearing. The light is beginning to break through. I will never go back to the husk of a man you called Papa, but who wasn't one."

The tears spilled over the dam of her lashes. "I've waited so long for this day."

"As have I. And I can't wait to hold you in my arms again, the way I did when you were little. I won't be able to throw you up in the air and make you laugh, but I can love you just as much.''

''I love you, too, Papa.''

''Sophie tells me she has made arrangements for a flight this afternoon. It will take a day for you to arrive, but—''

''No, Papa.'' Josie cleared her own throat, to drive the tears away. ''I'm not leaving here until I see Buck. I have to say goodbye.''

''Now, now, Joséphene. Surely you can live without your husband a day or two.''

''A day or...'' Josie froze. ''What do you mean?''

''Mr. Buchanan will be joining us in a few days. I really should get accustomed to calling him Hardin, I suppose, since he's my son-in-law.''

''Why would you have to get used to calling him anything?''

''You're married to him, Minette. Don't you remember?''

''Of course I do, but I can't—'' She broke off when she heard her father talking to someone else.

He came back on the line. ''I'm sorry. I have to go. The American president is on another line. I must thank him for returning you to me.''

''Papa, please! I need to—''

''I can't keep him waiting. He's been so helpful during the past week. I'll see you soon. Goodbye.''

''Papa!''

But a click cut him off the line.

Josie stared at the phone in amazement. She was going to stay married to Buck? How was that possible? Had they found gold on Montclaire?

''Princess?''

Josie blinked. ''Madame Angousset, do you know what my father's planning?''

The woman gently pried the phone receiver from Josie's fingers. ''You mean the wedding?''

"Wedding? What wedding?"

"Why, your wedding, of course. Prince Henri has been working day and night to—"

Josie grabbed her arm. "To whom am I getting married?"

"Why, Mr. Buchanan, of course."

"Buck? I'm already married to him."

Madame Angousset smiled and placed the receiver back in its cradle. "But you cheated the world out of a royal wedding. You must know how your papa feels about appearances. He wants to show the world that Montclaire can have as fine a wedding as any country."

"But we don't have any money."

"We will soon."

"How?"

"Why, your husband, of course."

"My husband?" Josie blinked again. This conversation wasn't making any sense. "Buck? What does he have to do with money? He doesn't have any."

Madame Angousset frowned. "You *are* married to Hardin Winford Buchanan II, aren't you?"

Josie thought back. "Yes, that was the name they put on the marriage certificate."

The older woman's lovely face cleared. "Then everything's fine."

Josie gave in to the very unprincesslike urge to scream. "Will you please give me a straight answer! What is going on?"

Madame Angousset pulled Josie onto the couch. She spoke plainly, but kindly. "If you had listened to the news, you might know. In four days, on your twenty-fifth birthday, you and Mr. Buchanan will repeat your vows in St. Béatrix Cathedral on Montclaire. That will make it official."

"I've deduced that. What I want to know is why. I thought I had to marry someone rich to save Montclaire."

Madame Angousset pulled back in surprise. "Why, Mr.

Buchanan is one of the wealthiest men in America, if not the world.''

"Rich?'' Josie's spine stiffened—an automatic response to the need to sink back against the couch cushions. "Buck is rich enough to save Montclaire?''

"Yes, indeed. He's already spoken with your father. You should hear the plans they're making for Montclaire.''

"He's talked with Papa? When?''

"This morning, Prince Henri told me.''

"I see.''

No, she didn't. Josie didn't "see'' anything. Her head was whirling so fast, she feared she'd faint.

"I'm afraid we must leave for the airport in three hours. Would you care to rest until then?''

Josie knew she'd never be able to sleep. She needed time to think, to gather information, to make some sense out of what she'd been told. "Could you please bring me all the newspapers you can find, and other publications that have articles about my marriage?''

"Are you sure you don't want to rest?''

"I've been out of touch so long, it will be more restful for me to know what's been happening in the world.''

"Certainly, Princess. I'll see that they're brought to you immediately.''

Josie let the magazine drop onto her lap and her head against the headrest of the private jet's seat. Was it lack of sleep making her thoughts swirl? Or jet lag?

Or learning the man she loved was an entirely different person than she thought he was?

Buck was no more a simple cowboy than she was a simple horse trainer. He was Hardin Winford Buchanan II—not one publication she'd seen had dared call him "junior.'' Son of Alicia and Hardin Buchanan, he'd been raised in a home worth several million dollars and was heir to a multimillion-dollar fortune.

Not that he needed it. Having graduated with honors from the Wharton School at the University of Pennsylvania with an M.B.A. in finance, he'd parlayed a modest inheritance from his grandfather into a fortune so vast, it made his parents seem like paupers.

The only way he could remotely be considered a cowboy was his ownership of the successful Double Star ranch in northeast California. That, and his halfhearted rodeo career.

The Buchanans were among the social elite of California, if not the United States. Mrs. Buchanan threw parties that presidents attended. The older Mr. Buchanan was very influential in politics. In short, they were as close to royalty as Americans could get, which made their son the perfect husband for her.

So why didn't that make Josie happy? She loved Buck, didn't she?

She closed her eyes with a ragged sigh.

How could she know? The man she loved didn't exist. He was a fantasy she'd made up—her cowboy in shining Stetson.

Of course, he'd fed her fantasy, lie by lie.

Oddly enough, the only link Josie felt to Buck was his rodeo career. Was it because that was the only persona she knew? Or was it because he used rodeo to hide from the world, just as she used her horses?

It didn't matter. One tiny link wasn't enough to base a marriage on, especially since that link meant their marriage would never work.

I'd never survive in your world. I'd hate it. Then I might begin to hate you, and that wouldn't be pleasant for either of us.

She remembered his words so clearly. What gave them the ring of truth was the way Buck lived—hiding from the world. The world that would now be avid for the smallest detail of his daily life.

He was being forced into this marriage. Josie was as certain of that as she was that one day he would hate her.

If they repeated their vows in St. Béatrix Cathedral, divorce would be next to impossible.

Somehow, she had to stop this wedding.

Chapter Eleven

Josie ignored the discreet knock on her bedroom door, hoping whoever it was would go away. She needed to think.

After a tearful reunion with her father, she'd slept eighteen hours straight. Since then she'd been out of her room only once, long enough to ascertain that because their marriage had been consummated, there was no stopping the wedding.

She smiled bitterly as she lay on a padded chaise longue angled toward the sun beating down on her balcony. Consummating the marriage had been her number-one priority—to save Montclaire, she'd told herself.

But deep down she knew the real reason had nothing to do with Montclaire. She'd wanted Buck with a hunger so acute, it was only assuaged when she lay in his arms.

She still wanted him that fiercely.

But the man due to arrive at any moment was not Buck. He was Hardin Winford Buchanan II. He and his family were flying in on the Buchanans' private jet.

Private jet. She couldn't believe only two days ago, she'd believed the only thing he traveled in was his beat-up truck.

Seconds later, a hesitant young maid appeared at the patio doors. "Mr. Buchanan has arrived, Princess. Your father requests that you join them in the east parlor."

"Thank you, Suzette."

Ten minutes later, Josie paused in the doorway of the east parlor. Her father sat on the ornate Louis XIV settee beside an elegant, dark-haired woman in a deep red suit. A distinguished older man sat on the matching chair to the woman's right. Buck sat in the chair next to her father.

Her eyes drank him in. He was familiar, yet not. Dressed in a custom-tailored dark gray suit, he looked more like a model than a cowboy. Or a successful businessman, which was what he really was.

Since he wore no cowboy hat, she could tell he'd had an expensive haircut since she'd seen him. It looked as if each hair had been cut separately so it would mold to the shape of his head.

He seemed like someone she'd met before, but couldn't quite recall where or when.

An apprehensive chill ran down her spine.

The instant he saw Josie in the doorway, Buck broke off the conversation with his father-in-law and sprang to his feet.

The discussion about the luxury resort he planned to build on the east side of the island could wait. He hadn't touched or even talked to his wife in three days, and he was desperate to get his hands on her.

Prince Henri followed Buck's gaze. He stood, which prompted Buck's mother and father to follow suit.

"Ah, Joséphene," Prince Henri said. "Finally. Come meet your husband's parents."

Damn the formalities. All he wanted to do was grab Josie and haul her to the nearest bed.

He watched his wife as her father introduced her to his

parents. Josie looked pale, tired, worried. The few glances she threw at him were too quick. She didn't look at all glad to see him. She looked...frightened.

Hell, he'd been afraid this was going to happen. He hated the way they'd parted—that she had to find out who he was from someone who didn't love her, who couldn't explain why he'd lied to her. And he'd been so busy setting the financial wheels in motion so he and Josie could take a long honeymoon that he hadn't been able to call her until the time difference between California and Montclaire made it—if not impossible, certainly rude.

Besides, he needed to explain in person.

When his mother began drawing Josie away, obviously wanting the new princess in the family all to herself, Buck put his foot down. *He* wanted Josie all to himself. He knew he'd only have a few minutes, but kisses were better than nothing.

"Sorry, Mother. Josie promised to show me her stables."

Josie's amber eyes met his in surprise. She'd never promised anything of the kind, thinking he'd never be on the island.

"Gracious, Hardin. How can you call Princess Joséphene something so...*intime*?"

Buck held his hand out to Josie. "Because that's my wife's name."

Josie's chin lifted. "What's yours?"

His voice dropped automatically. "To you, sweetheart, I'll always be Buck. Come on. I've been looking forward to seeing your thoroughbreds."

Her gaze lowered to his outstretched hand. She hesitated, then with obvious reluctance she placed her own in it.

Buck laced his fingers through hers and pulled her out the door. Instead of leading into a hall, it led into another room that looked identical to the one they'd just left. A small group of men gathered around a table in one corner glanced up, then quickly stood and kicked into formal bows.

Josie nodded at them distractedly.

Buck squeezed her hand. "You're going to have to lead the way. From what I've seen, this place is a rat maze inside a rabbit warren."

She pulled her hand from his and guided him through several more rooms, then finally into a hall. There were people working or talking in every room, and guards in the hallway.

Unable to keep his hands off his wife, Buck slipped an arm around her waist. "There's no privacy around here."

She didn't look up. "Not with all the preparations for the wedding."

"Why guards?"

She shrugged. "Partly tradition. But they're also here to stop…undesirables who try to slip into the palace."

"That's happened?" he asked in alarm.

"So far, only the odd reporter. One made it all the way to my bedroom once."

"I can see I'm going to have to install a state-of-the-art security system in this museum."

She stopped suddenly and looked up at him with a frown.

"What?" he demanded.

"It's strange, hearing you talk so casually about spending as much money as a security system for the palace would take."

He felt lower than the bugs found crawling under rocks. "I'm sorry, sweetheart. I was about to tell you when the bounty hunters busted in."

"I see." She started walking again.

"I mean it."

"All right."

He pulled her to a stop. "You have to believe me."

"I spent an entire week believing you. Now I discover

you're not the man I thought you were. I don't know what to believe anymore."

He frowned. "I'm not the only one who twisted the truth a little."

"I had a country to protect. What's your excuse?"

"Okay. I lied. Selfishly. I admit it."

"When you said you hated my world and wouldn't be able to survive in it—were you lying then?"

"Well…"

"Yes or no? It's not a difficult question."

He'd vowed he wasn't going to lie to her anymore. "No, I wasn't."

Her face seemed to fall into a thousand pieces, but she pulled herself together quickly, no doubt from years of practice. "You don't have to go through with this marriage, Buck."

Alarmed by her distance, by facing Joséphene instead of Josie, he grabbed her shoulders. "Yes, I do."

"Why?"

"Do you know how much work has gone into it in the past two days? Contracts have already been signed."

He could tell immediately it was the wrong answer. She struggled to be released, but he held her firmly. "I know you're angry, sweetheart, and you have every right to be. But we're married, and we're staying—"

"Princess Joséphene! There you are!"

"What the hell." He turned irritably to see an attractive redhead walking down the hall.

"What is it, Sophie?" Josie asked.

Despite his frustration, Buck admired the control of Josie's voice. No one would know they were in the middle of an argument.

"The seamstress is here, and so is your friend, Mrs. Denton. We must have the final fitting immediately for your dress and Mrs. Denton's if the alterations are to be done in time."

Buck saw a mixture of relief and irritation on Josie's face as she turned to him. "Please let me go."

He held on another second. "There will be no divorce, Josie." He released her and bowed formally. "If you'll excuse me, I'll find the way to the stables myself."

During a break in a meeting the next afternoon with the principality's top financial officers, Buck wandered over to a window looking out across the Mediterranean. Montclaire's Palais Royal had been built on the highest point of a white-faced cliff that stretched northward.

Somehow Buck had made it through the past twenty-four hours without letting on that he was going crazy. He hadn't seen much of Josie and when he did, they weren't given a chance to be alone.

Not that Josie wanted to be alone with him. That was obvious.

She turned the princess mode on whenever they were together. He couldn't find Josie beneath the Princess Joséphene facade, and it was tearing him apart.

Oh, she had stood beside him at the state dinner last night as they greeted dignitaries from all over the world, but she never addressed a single word to him. She had sat beside him at the press conference that morning, even smiled after he gave her a long kiss for the cameras.

But she was miserable. Though she schooled her features into a serene mask, he could see anxiety in the depths of her amber eyes.

Why?

The only reason he could come up with—the only thing that had changed between them—was his money. She'd discovered he was wealthy.

But why would she be angry because he'd turned out to

be rich? His money made him the perfect husband for her. She needed a rich husband, and she loved him. So why did she want out of their marriage?

He had no idea what reasoning was behind her decision, but he was determined to find out before tomorrow's wedding. He needed to get her alone, to make her talk to him, to hold her until she couldn't remember a time when his arms weren't wrapped around her.

Buck's eyes were tired from a sleepless night spent worrying about Josie's state of mind, and from looking at spreadsheets and financial projections since the state luncheon he'd spent beside his quiet wife. It felt good to focus them on the horizon.

His gaze swept up the coast, then back. Just when he was about to turn away, his eyes were caught by a movement on the cliff below. A slender woman with flowing black hair was riding slowly from the palace complex on a graceful white horse.

He knew the mare's lines from the tour of the stables he'd given himself the day before. More than instinct told him the woman on Alette's back was his wife. She wore blue jeans and a straw cowboy hat.

This was his chance to get Josie alone. Finally.

Josie raced Alette along the cliffs, feeling in control for the first time in four days. She'd walked out of a tea hosted by Melissa and her mother-in-law, unable to smile one more minute.

The familiarity of the path she'd ridden thousands of times during her life soothed Josie. As she rounded the curve that cut the palace from view, she slowed Alette to a walk. She was in no hurry to return to the battle she couldn't win.

As each day passed, she became more convinced Buck didn't love her. When they were together, he treated her like

Princess Joséphene, not Josie. There were no hello kisses, no subtle touching of her hand. Nothing to indicate he still wanted her.

Alette shied, but Josie reined her in easily, automatically.

Buck had more time for the financial concerns of the island than for her. He was closeted with her father, her father's advisors and the financial ministers of Montclaire every hour when there wasn't some state function to attend.

Contracts have already been signed.

It almost seemed that he wanted to stay married so he could invest in the island. But that didn't make sense. He could take Montclaire on as one of his little "projects" whether he was married to her or not.

She'd done more checking into Buck's financial background. According to her sources, he hadn't made his fortune in the stock market. The bulk of his money had come from providing capital to companies with a good product that didn't have the money to market it.

Montclaire might be considered such an invest—

The rumbling that was making Alette skittish finally penetrated her thoughts. Josie swung around in the saddle to see three small cars and two old farm trucks laden with people heading toward her. Cameras were already pointed her way. Between the depth of her thoughts and the pounding surf below, she hadn't heard the cavalcade until they were half a kilometer away.

Zut!

She'd been so anxious to leave the palace, she'd forgotten all about the media, and the long stretch of lonely shoreline north of the palace had lulled her into a false sense of security.

They'd obviously seen her leave and had commandeered whatever vehicles were available for pursuit. Reporters were crawling all over the island this week.

They were between her and the palace, so there was no escape. Nothing to do now but smile.

Groaning inwardly, she halted Alette and turned reluctantly to face them. Even though she was obviously not trying to get away, they came so fast and screeched to a halt so close to her, she barely kept Alette from backing over the edge of the cliff.

"Don't you people know anything about horses?" she yelled.

Her reprimand was drowned out by thirty voices screaming questions at her in God knew how many languages.

Suddenly, it was all too much. The week of being married, but not married. The belated wedding night. The callous "rescue" by the bounty hunters. Now the ordeal of a state wedding that would tie her forever to the man she loved—who would soon come to hate her. No one listening to her. No one caring that she was being torn apart.

Josie couldn't have answered a single question even if she'd been able to distinguish one from another. Feeling as fragile as a porcelain figurine, she sat ramrod-straight in the saddle, her eyes staring unblinkingly at the hills in the northwest that hid a wealth of marble. She desperately fought the misery that welled up inside her in the form of tears choking her throat, stinging her eyes.

She couldn't crack now. Not in front of this feeding frenzy. She'd lasted this long. Surely she could—

"I found you!" a familiar voice bellowed over the cacophony.

All eyes, including Josie's, turned toward a man sitting on a dancing white stallion at the back edge of the entourage.

Buck.

He'd come to her rescue, like a knight on a white steed. Except her knight was wearing a cowbot hat.

He easily handled her stallion, Bayard.

Josie didn't know whether the laughter threatening to break through her brave facade was gratitude or hysteria.

"But you made it too easy." He pushed his hat up a bit and grinned at her, ignoring the gaping media between them. "The noise alone would've led me straight here."

"Were you playing a game?" a reporter asked in heavily accented English.

"Or was she running away from you?" another added.

They all laughed—everyone but Josie.

Buck smiled good-naturedly and urged Bayard forward. The reporters parted for him like the Red Sea parted for Moses. He rode toward her slowly, calmly, his gaze locked on hers.

Josie saw concern in the depths of his blue eyes. Relief flowed through her veins like the first cup of coffee of the day. He did care for her.

He passed Bayard in front of Alette, circled around the back of the mare, then drew the stallion close alongside her.

All the while, cameras clicked and whirred.

When he was in place, Buck leaned over, braced himself with a hand behind her saddle and kissed her.

The reporters went crazy. Questions shot at Buck and Josie like bullets.

Reeling from the impact, she stiffened.

Buck drew away with a frown. "You okay?"

She barely heard the question above the noise. When the meaning penetrated, she nodded automatically.

Buck turned to the reporters and held up a hand for silence. He didn't speak until every last one of them shut up. "We'll do this in an orderly manner or we won't do it at all. Raise your hand and I'll call on you."

Every hand that wasn't holding a camera rose. Buck selected one.

"Is it true that your first marriage was never consummated?"

"None of your damn business," Buck answered matter-of-factly. "You there, in the gray shirt."

"Were you two having an affair before you got married?"

"None of your damn business. Next. You, with the long blond hair. Keep it clean."

"Are you sleeping together in the palace?"

"Is the princess pregnant?" another shouted out of turn.

Josie felt more blood leave her face with every question. The press conference at the palace had been carefully controlled. This was a mob, probing for blood.

Shaking his head in disgust, Buck threw a glance at her. He must have seen the panic on her face because he turned back to the reporters and began a monologue about the resort he was planning to build on the island. A few reporters shouted more personal questions, but he ignored them. Very quickly, others in the group realized what a scoop they were getting and hushed the unruly reporters themselves.

Josie was grateful when the questions turned from their sex life to Montclaire's economy, especially since they were all directed toward Buck. After a few minutes, she was able to breathe again—and listen.

At first, what her husband said seemed innocuous, but the more she listened, the more uneasy she became.

Buck became animated as he discussed his plans for bringing Montclaire into the twenty-first century. It wasn't until a reporter asked Buck what he stood to gain from the deal that Josie's skin began to crawl.

Buck threw a grin at Josie. "Beside the obvious?"

The reporters laughed on cue.

"If all goes halfway according to plan, the profits from my investments should be...substantial." The expression on his face was beaming, proud. Almost orgasmic.

Contracts have already been signed.

His words came back crystal-clear, and suddenly she remembered a quote she'd read in a newsmagazine. One of Buck's friends in college had said Buck once told him that making money was better than sex.

It's the most fun you can have with your clothes on, he'd told her that first day he taught her about investing.

The connections clicked in her brain, filling the previous gaps in her logic.

What had been bothering her was that Buck had refused to sleep with her because he was afraid they'd have to stay married. He'd resisted her "charms" for an entire week, then all of a sudden he'd come into the beach house intent on consummating their marriage.

The only thing different about that day was that he'd listened to the news for the first time. Obviously he'd heard something about Montclaire's financial troubles that made him think, then when she left him on the beach, he'd decided to take the island on as his latest project.

Betrayal pierced her heart like a knight's shining lance.

She was merely a part of the project. He hadn't made love to *her* that night, he'd made love to money.

Chapter Twelve

Horrified, Josie followed the path of her logic again, checking for flaws. There were none.

She held no temptation for Buck. That was as clear as the blue-green water off Montclaire's beaches. She'd offered herself to him with no strings attached, but he didn't want her until he'd discovered the financial opportunity she represented.

In other words, Hardin Winford Buchanan II was no different from Alphonse Picquet.

Josie rested her gaze on her husband, who was still talking enthusiastically about the money he was going to make—for Montclaire and himself.

When she could bear the sight no longer, she touched Alette with her heel and nosed into the crowd of reporters. Surprised, they parted for her.

Buck hesitated in his explanation of how many jobs the resort would generate for the island, then quickly began to end the interview.

Josie didn't care. When she was free of the mob, she urged Alette into a slow lope.

Buck and Bayard caught up with them halfway home. "I thought you'd be able to handle the press better than that."

Josie kicked Alette into a gallop. Bayard kept up easily with the mare, but the pace was too fast for Buck to give Josie a lecture on how to handle the media.

When they reached the stable, Josie didn't groom her mount as she usually did. She threw the reins to a startled stable boy and ran toward the palace.

Buck grabbed her arm and pulled her to a stop at the door. "What the hell's wrong with you, *Princess?* Trying to break both our necks?"

She jerked her arm away. "I'm sorry if you couldn't handle the pace. I'm familiar with the terrain."

He closed his eyes and mumbled, as if counting to ten. Then he opened them. "I need to talk to you."

"Open the door, please. I'm expected at the—"

"I don't give a damn where you're expected. I'm your husband. You can give me ten minutes of your precious time."

Josie felt the muscles in her jaw tighten. She threw a significant glance at the man guarding the portal. "Here?"

Buck took a deep breath—as if searching for control—then opened the door. "I'll walk you to your room."

She stiffened when he placed a hand on the small of her back, but instead of removing it, he slid it around her waist, obviously to prove he had the right.

"The way to handle the press," he said after a moment, "is not to show fear. They can smell it like a hound dog smells bird tracks."

She paused at the base of the stairs and looked up at him. "And what can you smell, Mr. Buchanan? You don't seem to care for the crown. It's the money, isn't it? Money is the only thing that means anything to you."

His eyes narrowed. "What the hell does—"

He cut himself off as a maid walked by with an armful

of linens. Grabbing Josie's arm, he hauled her up the stairs, muttering, "Damn this place. There isn't a single *solitary* corner in this entire mausoleum."

Josie didn't say anything until they reached the door to her room. Once there, she stopped and jerked her elbow from his grip. "I'll see you at the—"

"Wait just a damn minute. I'm coming in."

She straightened her shoulders. "This is my room."

"The wedding tomorrow means nothing, *Princess*. I'm already your husband."

Josie felt the heat drain from her face. She was afraid of this. He wanted to assert his husbandly rights. Though her body ached to throw herself into his arms and lose herself in his passion, she couldn't. He wouldn't be making love to *her*.

She lifted her chin. "Have a particularly good day with the finance ministers?"

He looked confused. "What the hell is that supposed to mean?"

Her hands clenched into fists at her sides. "I was naive enough to buy your lies before, but not anymore. You might be able to buy and sell my country, Mr. Buchanan, but you can't buy me."

He threw his hands in the air. "I'm not trying to b—"

"I have to stay married to you for Montclaire's sake. As a princess, I've had to do a lot of things in my life that I found personally revolting. But somehow I got through them. And I'll get through marriage with you. Somehow. But I won't—" Her voice cracked. "I won't be a real wife to you. I won't sleep with you again. Ever."

"What?" he roared, oblivious to the stares of the guards down the hall.

She kept her voice low. "You heard me. I won't settle for less than love. The time I spent with you taught me that.

If you want to stay warm at night, go sleep with your money.''

Taking advantage of the astonished look on Buck's face, Josie slipped into her room and closed the door. And locked it.

She leaned against the painted wood panels and gave in to the tears she'd been fighting for two days.

Her marriage was just beginning, but it was already over.

Frozen in stunned surprise by her words, Buck stared blindly at a chubby cherub grinning at him from Josie's bedroom door.

I won't settle for less than love.

Her words confirmed his worst fears. She had no interest in him now that she knew he was rich.

It would have been funny, if it didn't hurt so damn much. All the years of women who loved him only because he was rich, and he had to love one who fell *out* of love with him because he was rich.

To think he'd believed she loved both sides of him.

God, he was stupid. He'd learned years ago that he didn't fit into either high society's world or a cowboy's.

How the hell did he think he'd fit into a princess's?

Rage seared through him, fueled by betrayal.

He focused his eyes on the annoying little cherub.

He at least deserved to know why his money mattered so much.

Knowing a knock would be futile, he smiled grimly. Bashing in the door suited his mood so much more. Lifting a foot, he kicked. He didn't hit high enough to smash the cherub, but the wood around the knob splintered with a satisfying crunch.

Also gratifying was the choked-off scream that came from the other side. His wife was right to be afraid. He wasn't leaving until she'd told him everything he wanted to know.

When the guards began running down the hall, he glared at them. "Stay away from this door if you want to keep your jobs."

They knew who he was. He'd had a meeting with the security people to talk about installing a high-tech system, and to assure them they'd be trained to run it. His authority was moot now, but they didn't know that.

The guards nodded and went back to their posts, but threw uneasy glances over their shoulders.

Returning his attention to the door, Buck shoved it open and stepped inside.

Josie backed further away. "What are you doing? I demand you leave here at—"

"Demand all you want, *Princess*. No one will listen. The guards obey me now."

She glared at him. "Money buys everything, doesn't it?"

The arrow hit its target—his heart. "Apparently not."

Her face froze into its haughtiest, coldest princess mask. "Did you think you could buy love?"

"I thought I had your love before you knew I had enough money to buy anything. I thought I'd finally found a woman who loved me for all that I am. But you loved me only as long as you thought I was a poor cowboy. As soon as you learned I was rich, you had no more interest in me."

She appeared surprised by his insight, then indignant. "That isn't true."

"No?"

"No! I loved you when I thought you were poor and I love you now. Not that I want to." She winced, as if that admission caused her pain, but she continued bravely. "How much money you do or do not have has absolutely nothing to do with the way I feel about you."

Hope shot through him, but he tamped it down. "Then what's your problem? Why are you shutting me out?"

She took so long to answer, he thought she wasn't going

to. Then in a voice so soft he could barely hear her, she said, "Because you don't want me."

He blinked. "What?"

"You don't want me," she said, more loudly.

"Where the hell did you get that crazy notion?" he roared. "If I didn't want you, why would I be here?"

"Because you want the money." She eyed him cautiously, and her voice was little unsure.

"Money? What money? From what I've seen, you're on the verge of bankruptcy."

"The money you'll make from investing in the island."

Relief sank into his bones, so intense he almost collapsed. "Is that what this is all about? You think I'm marrying you to get money?"

She nodded hesitantly. "Why else would you marry me?"

When he stepped toward her, she backed up, so he halted. "I thought you were smarter than this. Think, Josie. What other reason could there be?"

She spread her hands. "I don't know. I've been trying to think of another reason, but there isn't one."

He shook his head. "All the centuries of inbreeding in European royalty has made you crazy. Could it possibly be that I love you?"

She looked stunned, as if that had never occurred to her.

He wanted to wring her neck, especially when she shook her head and said, "No. You're more interested in Montclaire's finances than in me."

"What the hell makes you say that?"

"You haven't even tried to kiss me since you arrived."

"If I haven't, it's because there's not a single place on this island where we can be alone—especially since someone decided we couldn't sleep together until after the wedding tomorrow. Your idea?"

She shook her head. "My father's."

"And in case you haven't noticed, I've been busy trying to get the ball rolling on Montclaire's economy so we can have a long, undisturbed honeymoon."

He took a step toward her. She stepped back.

"If you'll stand still, I'll rectify my little oversight right now."

"The money—"

"Sweetheart, I need more money like the ocean needs rain. It's true that I'm intrigued by the investments I'm making here. But not half as much as I'm intrigued by you."

He could tell she wanted to believe he loved her, but was trying to talk herself—and him—out of it. "But... I'm a princess, remember?"

He took another step toward her. "Your point?"

She stepped back again. "You hate high society. You've been running away from your parents' life-style since you were a little boy. The way I live is ten times worse."

"Can't argue with you there." Slowly but surely, he stalked her.

She backed away automatically, intent on her argument. "Not only do I have to attend tedious state functions filled with boring people who know nothing about horses, the media follows me everywhere. Cameras record everything I do. If I make one little mistake—if my slip is showing or I have spinach between my teeth—the world knows it."

"Don't you think I know that?" He was gaining on her. "Especially after today?"

"Buck, please give me a divorce. I don't want you to hate me!"

He stopped within an arm's reach, but didn't touch her. "Sweetheart, I should've kicked myself in the teeth to keep from saying that to you. I can tell you're going to worry about it—and worry me about it—the rest of our lives."

"Are you saying it isn't true?" she demanded.

"That's exactly what I'm saying. How could I ever hate

you? You're more precious to me than my own life. I love you, Josie. I always will."

"You love me?" she asked breathlessly.

"How the hell could you believe I don't? Would I be here if I didn't, enduring all the endless pandering and pampering that's ten times worse than merely being rich because I'm marrying into royalty? Enduring the smug satisfaction of my parents as they preen for the press and the guests? Sure, I enjoy the challenge of molding Montclaire's future, bringing the island out of the Middle Ages. But the only thing that has kept me sane was knowing I'd be with you, knowing I'll have you with me—in my bed—for the rest of my life."

Tears glistened in her beautiful amber eyes. "You want me?"

Buck reached out and drew her into his arms. His heart tumbled over itself when she came willingly, locking her hands behind his neck. He kissed her long and hard, savoring the fervor of her response.

The four days without touching her made his reaction to her instant. His hands pressed her hips into his, and he breathed against her ear, "What do you think? Do I want you?"

She pressed even closer, the witch, and smiled into his neck. "Yes."

"Even arguing with you turns me on. Everything you do, everything you say makes me love you more, makes me want you more. If you think for one moment you're going to get out of sharing my bed, then I'll just have to break down every door until you think differently. Wood centuries old is no match for a pair of steel-toed cowboy boots made in America."

"I love your cowboy boots," she said. "Promise you'll wear them tomorrow at our wedding."

He nodded. "I made a mistake, listening to my mother's

fashion advice. From now on, wife, you select my wardrobe.''

''Will you wear Wranglers and your cowboy hat to the ball tonight?''

''I will if you will.''

She giggled. ''Your mother and my father would choke on their champagne.''

''Do you care?''

She gave him a wry face. ''Yes. I suppose I'll have to wear a gown and you'll have to wear a tuxedo.''

''If you insist. Just promise me we'll wear nothing but Wranglers when we stay at our home in California.''

She sighed wistfully. ''Think we'll be allowed to go there sometimes?''

''I made sure it was added to the prenuptial. We get to spend at least four months out of every year at the Double Star.''

''We have another prenuptial?''

He shrugged. ''Things have changed since we signed the first one. We finalized the new one a couple of hours ago. It's waiting for your signature.''

She frowned. ''Are you sure you don't mind marrying a princess?''

He kissed the end of her nose. ''I'll get used to it.''

''What about the trailer-park queen you've wanted all your life?''

He hugged her close, chuckling. ''Sweetheart, you wear Wal-Mart panties. You may be a princess on the outside, but you have the heart and soul of a trailer-park queen— and that's the only thing that matters. It'll be my little secret, my way of laughing at the world that thinks it knows who you are.''

Josie liked the way he saw beneath the surface. ''You don't mind that you're pleasing your parents?''

''I'd be as crazy as you are if I let making them happy

get in the way of *my* happiness. And since the only thing that's gonna make me happy is gonna make them happy...well, I guess I'll get used to that, too."

Josie leaned against her husband with a soft sigh. "I don't know about them, but you've made me very happy."

He squeezed her close. "Have I, sweetheart?"

She nodded and raised her gaze to his. "You're the only man who loves me despite the fact I'm a princess, not because of it. You understand that though I have to be a princess sometimes, what I really want to do is train my horses."

He pushed a strand of hair from her cheek. "I understand you, Josie, because we're just alike. We both have two people inside of us."

She smiled and wrapped her arms around his neck. "I can stand to play princess if you're beside me."

"I'll be there. I promise. Every step of the way." He kissed her solemnly, then smiled against her lips. "And as we stand in the reception line at some ball or cut the ribbon on our fancy new resort, we'll smile at each other, knowing something the world doesn't—that the heirs to the throne of Montclaire would rather be mucking out stalls."

"I love you, my sweet investor-cowboy."

"And I love you, my beautiful princess-cowgirl." He kissed her. "Forever." He kissed her again. "For always." He kissed her deeply. "You'll be my one and only trailer-park queen."

Epilogue

One year later

"**Y**es!"

Josie slammed the phone into its cradle, shoved the rolling chair back from the desk and sprang to her feet. "Buck!"

She sped through the rooms of the sprawling Double Star ranch house, searching everywhere for her husband. "Buck, where are you?"

"I'm out here," she finally heard him call.

She stepped onto the back porch to find him carving a piece of oak. Happiness bubbled inside her as it always did at the sight of him. Or was it from the task he was lovingly performing? Or was it from her news?

"Guess what?" she asked.

"Well, you don't look depressed, so I know our time in California hasn't been cut short."

"Well, we have to leave for a few days, but when we return, we can stay a long, long time."

As she expected, he was surprised. "How long?"

"Indefinitely."

He stopped carving and gave her a doubtful look. "Sure. And old Ben the bull was just given a tutu and the lead in Sacramento Ballet's next production of *Swan Lake*."

She grinned at the image. "You'd better order box seats. I'm sure all the hands will want to see that."

He set his carving aside and held a hand out to her. "What gives?"

She walked to him unhesitantly and let him draw her onto his lap. "I just talked to Papa. I have some good news and some wonderful news."

"And the good news is…?"

"It seems Papa's been a naughty man."

"How so?"

She couldn't contain her grin. "Sophie's pregnant."

Buck leaned back. Josie could see the possibilities swirling in his clever head. She knew he'd already guessed what she was going to tell him, but all he said was, "Is that a fact?"

She answered him in the same laconic tones. "Yep."

"And the wonderful news…?"

"She's already had an amniocentesis. It's a boy."

A grin spread across his face. He knew exactly what those words meant. "We're off the hook."

He pulled her into a tight embrace, and she threw her arms around his neck. "We're free, Buck. Since succession is through the male line, my little half brother will be the poor, unfortunate heir to Montclaire, not us."

He hugged her tight, then drew back to smile at her. "I take it we're going to Montclaire for a hasty wedding?"

She nodded. "Very quiet. Just the family."

He regarded her skeptically. "No media?"

She rolled her eyes. "There's always media. But there's

not going to be a formal announcement until Papa and Sophie return from their honeymoon.''

He patted her stomach. ''Shall we tell them our news?''

She rubbed her hand across his. ''Let's not spoil their fun.''

''All right, sweetheart. We'll keep it to ourselves a little longer.'' He drew her closer to nuzzle her neck. ''Josie?''

''Hmmmm?''

''Want to go...muck out some stalls?''

She giggled. ''You do know how to turn a woman's head, don't you, Mr. Buchanan?''

He grinned. ''I know how to turn *my* woman's head.''

She raked her fingernails along his jaw. ''I'd love to muck out your stalls.''

He stood with her in his arms and headed inside.

''Oh, Buck.'' She pointed over his back. ''The stable's that way.''

''My stall's this way.'' He gave her a lecherous grin. ''I hope you've saved your strength, Mrs. Buchanan. You're gonna be mucking out my stall for a long, long time.''

She smiled and leaned her head on his shoulder. ''Is forever long enough?''

''It's a start, sweetheart. A very good start.''

* * * * *

If you enjoyed what you just read,
then we've got an offer you can't resist!

Take 2 bestselling love stories FREE!

Plus get a FREE surprise gift!

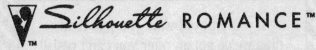

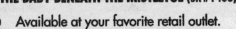

Start celebrating Silhouette's 20th anniversary
with these 4 special titles by
New York Times bestselling authors

Fire and Rain
by Elizabeth Lowell

King of the Castle
by Heather Graham Pozzessere

State Secrets
by Linda Lael Miller

Paint Me Rainbows
by Fern Michaels

On sale in December 1999

Plus, a special free book offer inside each title!

Available at your favorite retail outlet

V™ *Silhouette*®

Visit us at www.romance.net

PSNYT

COMING NEXT MONTH

#1408 THE BABY BENEATH THE MISTLETOE—Marie Ferrarella
Bundles of Joy
Natural-born nurturer Michelle Rozanski wasn't about to let Tony Marino face instant fatherhood alone. Even if Tony could be gruffer than a hibernating bear, he'd made a place in his home—and heart—for an abandoned child. And now if Michelle had her way, they'd *never* face parenthood alone!

#1409 EXPECTING AT CHRISTMAS—Charlotte Maclay
When his butler was away, the *last* replacement millionaire Griffin Jones expected was eight-months-pregnant Loretta Santana. Yet somehow she'd charmed him into hiring her. And now this confirmed bachelor found himself falling for Loretta...and her Christmas-baby-on-the-way....

#1410 EMMA AND THE EARL—Elizabeth Harbison
Cinderella Brides
She thought she'd outgrown dreams of happily-ever-after, yet when American Emma Lawrence found herself a guest of Earl Brice Palliser's lavish estate, he seemed her very own Prince Charming come to life. But was there a place in Brice's noble heart for plain Emma?

#1411 A DIAMOND FOR KATE—Moyra Tarling
The moment devastatingly handsome Dr. Marshall Diamond entered the hospital, nurse Kate Turner recognized him as the man she'd secretly loved as a child. But could Kate convince him that the girl from his past was now a woman he could trust...forever?

#1412 THE MAN, THE RING, THE WEDDING—Patricia Thayer
With These Rings
Tall, dark and *rich* John Rossi was cozying up to innocent Angelina Covelli for one reason—revenge. But old family feuds weren't sweet enough to keep the sexy CEO fixed on his goal. His mind—and heart—kept steering him to Angelina...and rings...and weddings!

#1413 THE MILLIONAIRE'S PROPOSITION—Natalie Patrick
Waitress Becky Taylor was tempted to accept Clark Winstead's proposal. It was an enticing offer—a handsome millionaire, a rich life, family. If only it wasn't lacking a few elements...like a wedding...and love. Good thing Becky was planning to do a little enticing of her own....